Rescue Me

Firehouse Blues Series: Book 2

AE Moran

Invisible Publishing Company

Firehouse Blues Series

Contents

Chapter 1: Leila

"Did you hear the one about the fireman who kept driving around town again and again without stopping?" Danny Brewer asks. "He was really burning rubber! Get it? Burning rubber?"

He nearly falls over himself laughing at his own joke and the rest of the fire crew joins in.

"I thought you were going to ask about the fireman who got a speeding ticket for driving the firetruck too fast," I tell him.

His brother Keith glares at Danny without even a trace of a smirk. "Is that the best you can come up with? It wasn't even funny."

"It's a firefighter joke," Danny counters. "See? Burning? Fire?"

Keith grits his teeth and the rest of us keep quiet when we see smoke billowing out of his ears.

Danny throws up his hands. "Forget it. I was just trying to lighten the mood."

"Do you have any other jokes, Danny?" my partner Chris Daniels asks.

"Don't ask him that!" Keith yells. "Don't encourage him."

The rest of us laugh again and turn back to the firehouse supply cabinets. "Did you get the extra IV bags?" I ask Chris.

"I got them.....but I don't see the spinal immobilization collars." She stands on her tiptoes to check the top shelves. "What am I missing?"

"You're checking in the EMS supplies. You're working on the rescue truck, remember? Extrication gear is in the next cabinet." I pull it open to show her.

She shakes her head and starts taking out collars and extra restraint straps. "It's gonna take me a while to get used to working on the truck. I've been on the ambulance for so long."

"Don't get used to it," Caleb Watts calls over from the linen cupboard where he's busy making up the ambulance gurney with new sheets and blankets. "John hired a new guy to take over as a paramedic on the truck. You'll be back on the ambulance pretty soon."

A groan goes through the crew. "No! Please, no!" Keith calls from the oxygen tank supply cage. "Not another new paramedic! I can't stand it."

"You're going to have to," I tell him. "John has to replace Ellen with somebody."

"How many is that we've been through so far?" Ellis Barrett asks.

"Four," Billy Cates replies.

"Five if you count that lady who only stayed for an hour before she left," Danny corrects.

"Is it us?" I ask. "Are we really that hard to get along with?"

"How can we be?" Naomi McPhee asks from the driver's compartment of an ambulance parked nearby. "We get along with each other. We all go out of our way to be nice to the new people....don't we?"

"I do," I reply.

"We all do," Keith tells me. "None of us wants to keep going through these new people like there's no tomorrow. We all want whichever new person John hires to work out so we can get on with our jobs."

"Be honest, man," Danny returns. "You scared them away by glaring at them. We all saw you, you big bruiser!"

He hooks his elbow around his brother's neck and tries to pull Keith in for a rough noogie on the head....which works out about as well as can be expected for someone as big, strong, and gruff as Keith Brewer.

He breaks out of his brother's hold easily, but he does it with such force that Keith trips and stumbles into me. His muscular bulk nearly topples me.

"Hey!" I yell and try not to drop all the medical supplies I'm getting out of the cabinet, but I lose my grip.

Packages of syringes, bandages, alcohol prep wipes, and a few oral airways fall on the floor at my feet.

Keith scrambles to catch me to stop me from falling, too. He grabs my arm, but his weight keeps falling against me so he winds up wedging his meaty arm against the cabinet behind my head to stop me from crashing into it.

He finally steadies me and keeps holding onto me while he looks at me at close range. "Are you okay?"

'I'm fine. Thanks."

"Let me help you with that." He bends over and helps me pick up all the fallen supplies. "You idiot, Danny! This is what comes from horsing around on the job. I should be making you pick this stuff up."

"I wouldn't be able to get near it with you in the way," Danny teases. "I can't even see the stuff. You're too big."

More laughter breaks out between the rest of our crewmates. Ellis starts to say something, but right then when Keith and I have our heads together near the garage floor, the deafening fire alarm goes off near the stairs.

It clangs through the firehouse and the crew freezes for a second before everyone races off to the trucks and ambulances.

Those of us who've been restocking the vehicles after our last call-out fumble to gather the last of our supplies. We can't leave without them in case the call turns out to be another medical emergency—which it almost certainly will.

I can't carry everything, but Keith doesn't leave. He scoops up the last items, cradles them in his arms, and hesitates long enough to make sure I get everything and don't drop anything. "You got it?" he asks. "Do you want me to take the airways?"

"I got it! Let's go!"

We both head for the rescue truck where the rest of the crew is already strapping into their seats. Danny, Caleb, and Ellis sit in the seats behind the driver's position where Billy is already firing up the engine. The garage door rolls up onto the ceiling to let the truck out.

Keith should be driving, but he's too busy helping me.

Danny sticks his head out through the window. "Hurry up! Quit playing the knight in shining armor! We gotta go!"

"Shut up, you jackass!" Keith roars, but he still doesn't leave.

He waits for me to get to the rear seat where Chris is racing to put away all the supplies before the truck pulls out of the firehouse.

Keith opens the door for me to climb in with my armload of goods. I dump everything on the seat and Chris has to scrape her stuff out of the way to give me room to sit down.

Keith adds his own load to the pile and slams the door behind him as he clambers in. "Go, Billy! We're in!"

Billy puts the truck in gear. Keith has to hold onto the seats and climb over his brother to get into the front passenger seat where he can direct Billy to the call.

Keith doesn't go out of his way to avoid stepping on Danny on his way past. In fact, I think Keith might actually go out of his way *to* step on Danny.

Danny hollers, "You big oaf! Watch it!"

Ellis and Caleb burst out laughing, but none of us has time to screw around right now. Keith shimmies into his turn-outs in between checking messages from dispatch and reading the map.

"The call is downtown!" he tells Billy. "Corner of Fourteenth Street and Howe Avenue."

Billy forgets to drive for a second and spins around to stare at him. "That's the Forsyth Bank building."

"I know!" Keith yells back and shoves his arms into the sleeves of his heavy protective jacket. "Police are on scene diverting traffic. They have the whole dang block cordoned off.

"What's the call?" Danny yells from the back seat.

"Gas explosion in the basement!" Keith replies over his shoulder. "You ladies hang back until we know the building is secure."

Chris and I are too busy putting all our gear and supplies away to answer. Rule number one of EMS is to never enter a scene until the firefighters and Police make sure it's safe. We don't want to become the next victims.

We don't get a chance to talk about the call before Billy swings the truck onto Howe Avenue, the main thoroughfare through town. Sirens echo behind us as the ambulances and John's support pickup pull into convoy behind the rescue truck.

We wind up driving into the Police cordon long before we get anywhere near downtown. Uniformed Police officers stand at every intersection and wave us through. Dozens of civilian cars and trucks stand parked on the side streets. They can't get onto Howe Avenue with the whole downtown area sectioned off.

Chris and I are the last two to get into our turnouts. Chris makes one last check of her drug box and I grab the jump kit so we're ready to deploy the minute the guys tell us it's clear.

The Police presence gets thicker and more ominous the closer we get to Fourteenth Street. The high concrete walls of office towers amplify the sound of dozens of sirens.

We don't need the siren anymore, so Keith switches it off as Billy pulls up in front of the Forsyth Building. The ambulances and support truck angle in next to us and we all jump out.

John Brewer, our fire chief, hustles over from the support truck and meets Jim coming from the other direction. "What's the status?" John asks.

"We're evacuating everyone from the building, but we need paramedics in there right away! A few of the maintenance guys got trapped in the basement when the explosion went off. They're too injured to walk out on their own and none of our guys have the training to deal with their injuries."

"How secure is the building?" John asks. "Did the explosion damage the structure?"

"That's what I was hoping you could tell us. We got some engineers coming over from the City Council, but we didn't want to send them in until you got here and took a look for yourselves."

"Where are the injured maintenance guys?" John asks.

"Over here. I'll show you." Jim Walker, the Police Chief, waves him forward, but at that moment, fifteen Police officers show up steering fifty people away from the building.

All the evacuees are wearing business attire. Some look terrified and cast frightened glances over their shoulders toward the building. Others are covered in dust and a few are bleeding from wounds on their heads.

John herds the fire crew out of the way to let everyone through. "EMS crew, take over dealing with these people," he orders. "Chris and Leila, you better come with us to check on these maintenance guys."

"What if the building is unstable?" Keith asks.

"Then none of you is going in, not even the fire crew. The maintenance guys will just have to wait until the City Council finds a way to stabilize the structure before we go in to get the patients out. I won't send the crew in unless it's secure."

I don't like the idea of leaving patients in harm's way, but I can't argue with his logic. John is the man. He would never put any of his crew in danger—not for anything.

As soon as the evacuees get to the ambulances, Jim leads John toward the Forsyth Building. The rest of us follow. Chris and I bring all our jump gear in case we meet any patients—whenever that turns out to be.

"The building looks fine from the outside," Keith remarks.

"The explosion was isolated to the basement," Jim replies. "None of the upper floors were affected at all."

"Why are those people bleeding, then?" I ask.

"Most of them either fell when the tremor shook the building or they got hurt trying to get out too quickly. A bunch of people panicked.....as you can imagine."

"I'll bet they did," Danny adds.

Jim leads our group into an alley between the Forsyth Building and the building next door, which is another office tower. We can see through the windows that it's empty, too. The Police have evacuated every building on the whole block just to be safe.

Jim stops in front of a plain steel door at ground level. "This is the entrance to the maintenance department in the basement. The injured guys are all down there."

"Are they alone?" I ask.

Jim shrugs. "I didn't want to leave my guys down there in case something went wrong."

"Did any of your EMT-certified officers assess the patients' injuries?" Chris asks.

"My boys didn't stick around long enough to check. I really couldn't tell you what you might be facing when you get down there."

John points to the door. "Open it up."

"It's open. You can go right in."

John hesitates for a second, studies the wall surrounding the door, and when he doesn't see any sign of cracks or other damage, he opens the door.

Chapter 2: Leila

John, Keith, Billy, and Caleb go into the basement first. Chris and I wait in the alley. I really wish I could go in there and check on the patients. Some of them could be critical. They could have been dying down there while they wait for us to show up.

A second later, Keith pushes the door open from the inside and sticks his head. "You two better get down here. The scene is secure and these guys are gonna need transport on the double."

He holds the door open for me and Chris to enter and then he races away to go get more people and equipment.

Chris and I descend a short stretch of concrete stairs to the basement floor. The walls look solid enough and we enter an open warehouse-style basement that covers most of the building's understory.

Massive concrete pillars hold up the rest of the building. The pillars all look strong and intact, too.

One whole corner of the building has been charred black by the explosion. It obviously originated in some kind of boiler or furnace in that corner.

What's left of the furnace lays open like a flower with the iron sides curling down and outward from the blackened center. Soot covers all the walls, ceiling, and pillars on that side, but the fire has long since blown out.

"Over here!" John calls and Chris and I hustle over to where he, Caleb, and Billy bend over six maintenance guys lying on the floor.

One of them is already dead. He's been cut in half by a piece of flying metal blown out of the furnace. The fragment sticks out of his back like a shark's fin. We don't go near him. The coroner will deal with him.

One of the other guys sits against the wall with another massive fragment of torn metal lying across his legs. He babbles endlessly while John tries to calm him down.

"I gotta call my wife, but my phone is in my pocket! You gotta get this off me so I can get my phone. I gotta call my wife! I'm supposed to pick up my son from school today and meet my daughter at the house when she gets off the bus. My wife will kill me if I'm not there!"

"Take it easy, man," John tells him. "We'll call your wife for you. Don't worry about it. I'm sure she won't be mad when she finds out what happened."

"You don't know her, man!" The guy starts to lose it. He's obviously in shock and not thinking clearly. "The teachers at my son's school get really snotty if parents are late to pick up their kids. What will my kids think if I don't pick them up?"

"Don't worry about it, brother," John tells him again. "We can send Police officers to pick up your kids. We have bigger things to worry about right now."

He shoots me and Chris a look over his shoulder and we split up. Chris goes over to the guy with the crushed legs. I don't even want to know what his legs look like under that slab of four-inch steel.

I go over to the other four guys. Two of them are unconscious. One of them has burns all over his face and the other's clothes have been completely torched off. He looks like he's got burns over most of his body, but both of them have normal pulse and respirations.

I turn to the last two guys. One of them lies on his back, but he's definitely wide awake and in excruciating pain. I can't see what's causing it.

Billy and Caleb work overtime to hold the guy down while he thrashes, bellows, and tries to fight them off.

Billy has to yell to make himself heard over the guy's thunderous raging. "You gotta lie still, man! You're hurt! You could wind up dead if you don't keep still."

"Can you see what's wrong with him?" I yell to Billy over the noise.

"Are you insane?" he fires back. "*You* try to see what's wrong with him."

I can't get near him with the guy struggling so badly, so I turn to the last guy. He sits in the middle of the floor at a distance from the others. His shoulders slump and he looks down at his hands in his lap.

I don't see anything wrong with him, either....except for the way he sits there bowed and silent while his friends are either dying or raging from their injuries.

I go over to him and touch his shoulder. "Are you okay? Are you hurt?"

He looks up very slowly. He's a youngish guy—maybe mid-twenties. He has deep, sea-green eyes and he blinks extra slowly when he sees me. "Something's wrong."

"What's wrong?" I ask and bend a little closer so I can hear him over the other guys' yells.

Fortunately, right then, Keith comes back with Danny, Andy Skinner, Naomi, and a whole crap load of extrication equipment.

Andy and Naomi go over to help Billy and Caleb restrain the struggling guy. Danny approaches John, and right then, Sophie McNish shows up and starts working on the guy with the crushed legs.

She directs John and Danny to get on either side of the plate to lift it off the patient's legs.

"Something's wrong." The guy in front of me draws my attention back to him, but I can see that he isn't trying to get my attention at all. He doesn't even seem to be aware of me.

He blinks again like he's completely out to lunch. I squat down and open my jump kit to start doing an assessment on him. "What's wrong? Are you in pain anywhere? Did you get hit by the blast?"

"Something's......wrong." He draws a massive sigh between the two words and his eyes don't track when I move to his other side. Something is definitely wrong. I just don't know what it is.

He might have gotten thrown against the wall and suffered internal injuries. How would I know? Finding out what's wrong with him is going to be difficult if he can't tell me what it is.

I take his vitals. They're all within the normal range except that his heart rate is very slightly elevated—not enough to concern me. He might just be recovering from the explosion.

I shine my flashlight in his eyes. His pupils are perfectly reactive—so why is he so out to lunch?

"Could you squeeze my hands for me?" I put my fingers between his fingers, but he doesn't squeeze.

"Something's wrong," he tells me again.

"I know," I reply. "I'm gonna find out what it is and we're going to get you out of here. I promise. Can you take a deep breath for me?"

I press my stethoscope to his chest, but he doesn't take a deep breath. He doesn't even hear me.

He has to breathe to say, "Something's wrong," again and his lungs sound clear. I can't for the life of me figure out what *is* wrong with him.

I finally start doing a physical examination. I pat down his head, neck, shoulders, arms, chest, sides, stomach, and back.

He doesn't move through the whole exam until I get to his back. I prod down his spine and he winces when I touch him near his waist. "Does that hurt?" I ask.

"Something's wrong," he tells me and I definitely hear a tremor in his voice. Whatever is wrong with him must be in his back.

"I need you to unzip your coveralls so I can check your back," I tell him, but he still doesn't respond except to blink at me again in that slow, dull way of his. I have to work quickly before the shock catches up with him and he crashes on me.

I unzip his coveralls. He half-heartedly helps me by shrugging out of his sleeves, but he barely moves the rest of his body.

Now that I notice it, he doesn't seem to be moving his legs much if at all. I'm starting to get a very bad feeling about this.

I tug his coveralls down to his waist. He's wearing a plain white T-shirt underneath. I move around behind him and lift the shirt.

My blood runs cold when I see a perfectly straight, two-inch bruise cutting horizontally across his back right above his hips. The purple welt stands out against his white skin.

The bruise bisects his spine right at waist level. This is bad. This is beyond bad. Something must have hit him there. It could have severed his spinal cord at waist level. That must be why he isn't moving his legs.

I stare at the bruise for a minute and then snap out of my trance. "I need a bunch of extrication equipment over here!" I yell across the basement. "This patient needs immediate transport!"

Billy, Caleb, Andy, and Naomi are busy carrying their struggling patient out of the basement. Sophie, John, and Danny have their hands full fitting a MAST suit to the guy with crushed legs. I'm on my own here.

I scramble over to my jump kit and work overtime to get out an IV bag and tubing. This guy is going to crash. It's only a matter of time. It's a miracle he's still sitting up with his eyes open.

"Something's wrong," he tells me again.

"I know," I gasp. "I'm gonna take care of you. I promise. The fire department is right outside. We're going to take you to the hospital. I promise. Just....try to stay calm....."

He's staying perfectly calm. I'm the one freaking out.

I glance over my shoulder. When will the crew come back to help me?

"Would you mind lying down on your back?" I ask my patient. I don't want him to fall over when the adrenaline wears off and he finally passes out.

"Something's wrong," he tells me.

"Yeah, okay. Nice and easy. I know your back hurts. Just....lie dow n....."

I take him by the shoulders and slowly, very slowly ease him backward onto the floor. He cooperates perfectly, but as soon as I get him into that position, his eyes lose focus. "Something's wrong."

I don't answer this time. I have to work fast to start the IV and get him on some oxygen.

I'm just opening my drug box when the basement door slams open. Keith and Billy come back with a backboard and some more immobilization equipment. My heart sinks when they go over to Sophie and Danny.

John stands up, says something to the others, and heads back toward the door. None of them is coming near me for a while.

Billy puts the backboard on the floor and angles it closer to the guy with crushed legs. He's still babbling about calling his wife, so the MAST suit must be working. He's still conscious.

Keith glances over at me and our eyes meet. Danny and Billy will need his help to carry the other guy out of the basement. How long after that will they come back for my patient?

Keith glances down at the guy with crushed legs and I see the puzzle pieces click in Keith's mind as he realizes. Then he glances toward the door. Please Dear God in Heaven let him be thinking of going out there to get some more people to help me.

I can't keep looking at him. I start to turn back to my patient when Keith yells, "Look out!"

I don't have time to turn around. I see him out of the corner of my eye as he charges across the basement impossibly fast.

Before I know what's happening, he collides with me in a flying tackle, slams me away from my patient, and Keith's iron, muscular arms lock around me as we both somersault across the floor.

We roll against the opposite wall just as the ceiling caves in right on top of the guy I've just been working on. A massive avalanche of concrete, torn reinforcing bars, and debris smashes into the floor and completely cut off me and Keith from the rest of the crew.

I scream and duck my head. Keith wrenches his body over on top of me and a bunch of sharp boulders pound onto his back. He tucks his head and covers me with his body, but I can still hear him roaring in pain as the rock hits him.

The noise overwhelms everything for a second and then dead quiet descends over the basement. I don't dare to open my eyes until Keith pries his head up.

He looks around, coughs, and then squints his dark brown eyes at me through clouds of dust. "Are you okay?" he yells.

I nod fast. Dust clings to his shaggy, sandy-brown hair, beard, and skin. He coughs again and then spits to one side to get dust out of his mouth.

"Are *you* all right?" I gasp. "Let me take a look at your back."

Keith slowly pries himself off me and then bellows when he tries to move, but at least he *is* moving. He pivots onto his knees, stretches his shoulders, and grimaces. "Damn it! That hurt!"

"Did you get hit in the head?" I struggle to sit up and look around. "My kit is under that pile. I don't have any gear."

"It could be worse." He rubs the back of his neck and dust falls into his eyes. "Jesus! I didn't see that coming!"

"You did see it coming." I move over next to him. "What happened? Pull up your shirt so I can see your back."

He pulls up his uniform shirt, but he's obviously more interested in looking at the mountain of rubble in front of us than whatever happened to his back.

He peels his shirt up to his shoulders and displays the wide expanse of muscle underneath. Thick straps of muscle around his shoulder blades glide under his smooth skin when he pulls his shirt out of the way.

I examine his back. "You just have a bunch of bruises—nothing serious."

"I could have told you that," he replies over his shoulder in his gruff way. "You don't have to make a fuss over me."

I swivel around in front of him. "Yes, I do. Thank you. You saved my life."

"What are crewmates for, right?" He shoots me a grin and then squints up into the giant crater leading to the building's ground floor. "Now the question is how do we get the hell out of here."

"Keith!" Danny yells from somewhere out of sight. "Are you over there? Leila! Are you all right?"

"We're here!" Keith calls back. "We're fine, just......you know.....trapped."

"Stick tight," John chimes in. "We're gonna get you out."

Keith snorts and mutters under his breath. "Like we could go anywhere if we wanted to. It looks like we're missing the firehouse procedures meeting this afternoon."

I have to laugh. "Dang. What a shame."

He chuckles and grins at me again. "Sorry I didn't get to you sooner. I should have helped you."

"You probably wouldn't have seen the building losing stability if you had been helping me. What happened? How did you know the ceiling was going to cave in just then?"

"I just looked over at you and that's when I noticed the cracks shooting across the ceiling. It was pure luck."

"Thank you so much," I exclaim. "That was one of the most heroic saves I've ever seen in the service."

He makes a face. "You can stop that now. I didn't do anything."

I want to insist that he definitely did do something, but insisting will only make him uncomfortable. I've known Keith Brewer for years and he's one of the humblest firefighters that ever lived.

He can't stand anyone making a big deal about him doing his job. He always goes the extra mile, though I can't say I've ever seen him do anything as impressive as what he just did for me.

He never thinks what he's doing is a big deal. He lashes out at anyone who tries to praise him. That's what makes him such a hero. He doesn't even know he is one.

He sits down on the floor and snarls again when he leans his back against the wall. "I guess we just hurry up and wait. Aarrgh!"

"Maybe you should go to the hospital if you're in that much pain," I suggest.

"Don't ever let me hear that word coming out of your mouth again," he growls.

I laugh. "What—hospital?"

"What did I just tell you? That word is banned."

I laugh a little more and then sit down next to him. "We could be here for a while."

"Too bad about your boy. What was wrong with him?"

"Fractured spine. He might have had a severed spinal cord.....and internal injuries. I guess it doesn't matter now."

He turns around and peers at me extra hard. "Are you okay? I know how much it sucks to lose patients."

"I'm okay. Thanks for asking." I slip out of my turnout jacket. It's getting hot in here and I don't need it anymore.

Just then, Danny sticks his head over the side of the hole above us. "Hey! Are you two ready for the management meeting yet?"

"Go away!" Keith yells back. "We were just about to have lunch."

Danny laughs. "It's time to go! Come on. We're getting you out of there." He twists his neck downward to survey what's left of the basement. "No patients....or anybody?"

"No," I reply. "The only patient is under that pile of rubble now."

He shrugs that away. Keith frowns up at him. "What are you doing, man? You can't be on the ground floor. You're too high."

"The building is too unstable. We're bringing in a crane to lift you out. Billy will come down with the rescue basket. Stand by a sec." He vanishes.

"Rescue basket!" Keith mutters. "My life is over, now that I have to ride in the rescue basket."

"Things could be worse, right? You could be going to the......" I break off and giggle when he shoots me a dangerous look.

"Watch it," he tells me and then we both laugh. Today wouldn't be the first time Keith has had to go to the hospital in the line of duty.

The noise of machines makes us look up as a giant crane arm extends into the building beyond the breach above our heads. It purrs as it slides out one nested arm after another.

It locks into place with Billy dangling in the rescue basket at the end. He grins at us and then waves to someone out of sight to direct the crane driver where to position the arm.

The crane motors downward and the basket descends through the breach until it touches the floor. Keith and I clamber into the basket. "Are you saving the day again?" Billy asks Keith.

"Shut up!" Keith growls and Billy laughs. Keith's exploits are already legendary. They'll be getting downright epic after today.

We climb in and Billy hollers, "Take it up!" through the hole.

The crane lifts and carries the three of us outside into the sunshine.

Chapter 3: Keith

I definitely feel the bruises on my back when I twist around to reverse the firetruck into the firehouse garage. Every move hurts, but it was worth it.

The rest of the crew won't stop talking about me tackling Leila out of the way when the ceiling collapsed, but at least the crew is mostly turning it into a joke.

Fortunately for my sanity, she does the same thing.

"You should have stayed under the pile of rocks," Ellis tells her when we get out of the truck. "It would have been lighter than having that lump landing on top of you."

"Softer, too," she jokes. "And not so bristly."

The others laugh, but I can take it on the chin. It's all in good fun.

We hang up our turnouts and the paramedics start to resupply the trucks and ambulances. "I'll need a new jump kit," Leila remarks.

"Good luck getting John to approve that," I tell her. "You know what he's like when it comes to expenses."

"I'm guessing he doesn't want to salvage the one I lost in the building," she replies. "My whole IV rig and oxygen setup were in that kit."

"You should probably make a report to the Police Department," I point out. "Your drug box was in it, too. If they recover the dead guy's body, the drugs will be exposed. The Police will want to take those into custody."

"Good idea." I catch her smiling at me. "Thanks. I didn't think of that."

I'm just about to tell her to stop thanking me for every little thing when John comes in. He isn't wearing his turnouts anymore. He's in full Fire Chief garb, which means he probably just finished having a meeting with Jim and the Police Department about the call.

"I need you two to fill out an incident report on the building collapse," he tells me and Leila.

"No problem," I reply. "Do you want that now?"

"Listen to this guy!" Danny chimes in. "He just got pulverized by a collapsing building and he can't wait to fill out the paperwork....and don't give any static about how you're just doing the job. You are ten thousand percent firefighter, man. Whoo! I have never met anyone as enthusiastic as you."

I'm just about to tell him for the hundredth time today to put a sock in it when someone calls from behind us. "Good work out there today, folks. Decorations all around."

The whole crew turns to see who it is as Damon Cassidy walks through the garage doors. He's still wearing his Police uniform.

The crew all calls out greetings to him. Damon is a fixture around the firehouse. "Hey, buddy! I didn't see you at the scene," Billy replies.

"I was on the north end of Howe Avenue. A bunch of family members came over there and they were kicking up a fuss about getting through to find their loved ones." He turns to Leila. "Are you ready to go, babe? Your shift ended half an hour ago."

"Yeah. Just let me...." She glances at the other paramedics. They're all crowding around the supply cabinets.

"Just go," Chris tells her. "I'll handle it."

"Thanks." Leila shoots all of us her winning smile.

Concrete dust still clings to her curly, gold-tipped auburn hair and the same dust covers her uniform, but she still looks stunning. Her blue eyes sparkle as brightly as ever and her bubbly, vivacious personality shines through everything.

Damon is a lucky guy, and from the way he's walking out of the garage with his arm behind her back, he knows it.

I turn back to my crewmates and start wrapping up the restraint straps we used to carry the other maintenance guys out of the basement. We used every piece of extrication equipment we have on that call and we didn't even save everybody.

It sucks that we lost Leila's patient. I sure hope she isn't too broken up about it. I know how the paramedics carry these things around with them.

I pop the equipment box on the side of the ladder truck to put the straps away when John comes over to me. I know my brother, but anyone on our crew would be able to see that I-mean-business look coming a mile away.

"Can I talk to you in my office for a sec?" he asks me.

"Um....sure." I shut the equipment box. I'm getting dragged up to John's office, which means I won't be coming back anytime soon.

The others all notice and they stop what they're doing to watch me head off to my own funeral. John might be my older brother and my best friend, but he's still my boss.

It would be a cold day in Hell before he took it easy on me or Danny just because we're his brothers. If anything, he's harder on us than he is on anyone else precisely because we are his brothers. He can't let anyone think he plays favorites.

He steps behind his desk, but he doesn't sit down nor does he tell me to sit down. He fixes me with his hard, black eyes. One look from that guy can cut through solid steel.

"You okay?" he begins. "Did you get hurt at the scene?"

I try to shrug it away. "I'm all right. Leila took a look at me right after it happened, but I'm all good. What is this about? Is there a problem?"

"How did you know the ceiling was going to collapse when it did?"

"Oh, that. Billy and I were coming back downstairs and we took the backboard and stuff over to you and Danny and Sophie. Billy squatted down so we could load up Sophie's patient and then I noticed Leila working on that other guy across the room."

"Yeah?" he asks. "What about it?"

"Well, she gave me this kind of pleading look like she needed help, but I didn't feel right about just walking away when Danny and Sophie obviously needed me to help them carry out their patient. I wasn't sure what to do, so I looked back up at Leila….and that's when I saw the cracks shooting across the ceiling. A few pieces of concrete came loose and the cracks kept spreading way faster than they should have and then….well, I guess I just reacted. The fall was already starting to happen right on top of Leila and her patient…..so I just did it…..See?"

"So you didn't see any sign before that to indicate that the basement might be unstable? Was that the first you saw?"

"No! I mean yes! Of course I didn't see any sign before that! I would have told you! I would have told all of you! You know that! I wouldn't have gone into the basement myself, much less let any of the crew go down there if I did see anything. Wait a minute. You don't think…..?"

I break off and point at him. I can't say the words. He better not suspect me of keeping information like that from him.

"Of course not," he replies, "but I wouldn't be doing my job if I didn't ask. We lost a patient and we could have lost Leila."

I slump and let out a shuddering sigh of relief. "Don't remind me."

"You did great out there." He sits down in his chair. "You can go....unless there's something else you wanted to talk to me about."

"You mean.....that's it? I'm not in trouble?"

"Why would you be in trouble? You saved Leila's life."

"You mean.....?" I can't stop staring at him. I can't believe he isn't ripping me a new one, although I can't think what he would be ripping me a new one for.

He makes a show of looking at his watch. "You're off duty now, aren't you? Are you going home or do you have plans for tonight? Why don't you come over for dinner?"

I open my mouth, but it still takes me a minute to understand that the confrontation is over. "No, I.....I don't have any plans."

"So do you want to come over? I'll text Ellen that you're coming."

"Um....okay." I glance over my shoulder. Should I just....leave—just like that?

"Great. So I'll see you later."

I nod at nothing and leave the office in a daze. I really thought I was in for it that time.

By the time I get back downstairs, the crews are all on board the trucks putting stuff away, cleaning up, and organizing their equipment for the next call. None of them sees me clock out and head for the garage door.

It's only four o'clock in the afternoon and blazing sunny outside. I still have hours of daylight left before I go over to John's house for dinner.

I turn toward the parking lot and the hair stands up on the back of my neck when I hear voices coming from behind the firehouse.

They aren't coming from the parking lot. They're coming from the other direction—from behind the building where no one should be.

"Do you think I'm blind?" a male voice snaps. "Do you think I'm stupid? Is that what you're saying? Are you really going to stand there and tell me to my face that I'm too stupid to understand what's going on right in front of my eyes?"

"I wasn't saying that at all, Damon!" Now I recognize Leila's voice, but I don't recognize her tone. I've never heard her talk like this—ever—to anyone. "I wasn't...."

"I saw you with my own eyes, you stupid tramp!" Damon fires back. His words cut like a knife. "Why don't you just go out on the street corner and sell your body to any loser who will pay for it? You'll make more money than you do working here."

"I wasn't doing anything, Damon!" she cries and her voice cracks. "I swear! I was just....."

"You're a traitorous bitch!" he snarls. "That's what you are. You're going behind my back, and as soon as I find out who the other guy is, I swear to Christ, I'll make sure he pays for it the same as you."

"Damon......" I can't see what they're doing behind the building, but the next minute, a scuffle breaks out and I hear what sounds like a smack followed by Leila crying out again.

No way in hell will I stand around listening to that. I step around the building and walk up on him holding her by the arm above the elbow.

He clamps his fingers around her arm tightly enough to hurt her. My blood starts to boil, but I keep it on a tight leash.

I always liked Damon Cassidy. I always thought he was a good guy and a good cop.

That's what I thought before today, that is. All of that goes out the window when I see him manhandling Leila.

I've worked with her for years. She's part of the firehouse family. No way would I ever let any piece of trash lay his hands on her like this. Uh-uh.

"What's the problem?" I ask as calmly as I can.

Damon turns on me with a vicious snarl. So now the mask is off now and he doesn't try to hide his dark side anymore. "Is it you?" he snaps. "Are you the one?"

"The one what?" I ask.

"Stop it, Damon!" Leila shrieks. Her voice spikes in pain, fear, and anger. That sound shoots straight through me. She's scared of this prick—and he's hurting her. "I'm telling you I didn't do anything!"

Damon ignores her and bares his teeth at me. "If you're him, you better back the hell off before something bad happens to you."

I raise one eyebrow at him. "Are you threatening me, man?"

"Damon—!" Leila yells again.

He rounds on her, yanks her over to his Police cruiser sitting at the curb, rips open the passenger door, shoves her inside, and slams the door before he comes marching back over to get in my face.

"Let's get one thing real clear right now, pal," he hisses through locked teeth. "Leila is mine. Understand?"

"It looks to me like today is the very last day you can say that—*pal,*" I sneer. "You just shit in your own bed and you're too stupid to know it. She actually cared about you enough not to tell you so to your face, but I will. You're a slobbering idiot if you treat a girl that nice the way you just did."

He steps right up to me and jabs his finger in my face. "I knew it! You're the one, aren't you? I knew it was someone from the firehouse."

"The one what?" I ask again, but I'm already starting to get the picture.

"You've been screwing around with her behind my back! Don't think I don't know what goes on in here when she stays late and says she's on a call."

I frown at him trying to wrap my head around the sheer epic moronitude of what he just said. Then I burst out laughing. "You're a cop, you dipshit. You can hear on the radio when she goes out on calls and when she comes back. Are you that paranoid that you don't hear what she's doing?"

He doesn't soften in the slightest. He points in my face again. "You stay away from her. Understand? Don't make me have to put you down."

Now I raise both eyebrows. "Put me down? You think *you* can put *me* down?" I drag my eyes very slowly down his body and back up to his face.

He's a big guy and he obviously takes care of himself. He's as tall as I am. He might not be as strapped in the shoulders, but I bet he can hold his own in a fight.

There's one thing he'll never have on me. I can get mean when someone pushes me too far. That's why I don't let myself lose control of my temper. I learned that lesson young and now I don't go there.

I used to think he was strong enough to handle himself when the fur starts flying. Now I know better about that, too.

If he's out here pushing his woman around and hurting her in public, then he's nothing but a coward. He takes out his aggression on women because he can't stand up to real men.

If it comes down to brass tacks between me and this pipsqueak, I'll mop the floor with him and we both know it.

He points at me one more time, mutters, "Don't say I didn't warn you. You stay away from her," and stalks off to his car.

He gets into the driver's seat, starts the engine, and drives away. Leila doesn't look at me and then the car turns a corner and disappears.

Chapter 4: Leila

I sit in my car for a long time and do everything possible to get my heart rate to calm down. I eye the firehouse across the parking lot. I'm already late for work, but I can't bring myself to go in there.

I never thought I'd live to see the day when I would dread going to work at the firehouse. I love the place and everyone in it. How did I let Damon corner me into this? How did I let him rob me of the one thing I love most in the world?

I can't let him get away with this, but it's too late. He already has gotten away with it and now Keith knows about me and Damon.

I've been going out with Damon for a year and we've always managed to keep everyone in the dark about what our relationship is really like. Everyone thinks we're the perfect couple.

Now that's gone, too. How can I face Keith, now that he knows?

I've always been one of the few people who could make him laugh. He doesn't have to tell me I'm one of the people he's most comfortable with. He shows it in everything he does around me.

Now Damon has taken that away from me, too. I work with Keith on the same truck, on every call. We work together all day every day. I won't be able to escape him.

Has he already told John about me and Damon? That's exactly the kind of thing Keith would tell John—and why shouldn't Keith tell

John? It affects one of John's employees, and by extension, the whole crew.

I cringe at the thought of John finding out. He and Jim work hand in hand. They see each other practically every day. Anything untoward that might be going on with firehouse personnel affects the Police Force, too, especially when Damon is a cop on the Force.

I struggle to pull myself together. I have to go in there or at least explain to John why I'm missing work.

Right then, Sophie comes out of the garage, frowns toward the parking lot, and sees me sitting behind the wheel of my car. I can't delay any longer—not when people are coming out here to look for me.

I get out of the car, lock the door, and plaster a fake smile on my face as I walk toward her. "Good morning."

She frowns even more deeply. "Are you okay?"

"I'm fine. I just got a really important email from my mom, but it's all taken care of now."

I walk past her and she follows me into the garage. The rest of the crew is busy going through morning checklists, inventorying supplies on all the vehicles, and calling jokes across the garage.

No one sees me go to the locker room to put my stuff away. Sophie goes back to work.

I take as long as possible to hang my stuff in my locker, but I can't fall into the trap of hiding in here for the entire shift. People would definitely notice that.

I take my uniform jacket out of my locker to put it on, but just as I'm closing my locker door, I hear another door close behind me.

I spin around fast and the bottom drops out from under me when I see Keith shutting the locker room door with himself and me alone inside.

I freeze....and then my nerves crumble the rest of the way into full-blown hysteria when he turns around and I see the look in his eyes. He knows. Neither of us can hide from it anymore.

"Are you okay?" he asks in his deep, rumbly voice. "I don't know why I even ask that. Of course you're not okay. Why didn't you tell me—or John—or any of us? We could have helped you. We still can help you."

I do my best to wave that away. "It isn't what you think...."

"Oh, it's definitely what I think." He strides over to me, but I can see now that he doesn't come too close. He never would have kept his distance like that before. "Did he slap you right before I walked around that corner? Is that what I heard—a slap—or was it something more?"

I raise both hands and then let them drop in defeat. What's the point in lying about it? Keith is too smart not to realize just how far this nightmare has gone between me and Damon.

"Just.....just drop it, okay?" I hear how cringing and pathetic my voice sounds. I sound nothing like I usually sound at the firehouse. This place usually makes me feel confident and sure of myself.

He compresses his lips and his eyes flash. I know that look. He's angry. He's more than angry. He's mad as hell and you don't want to get in Keith Brewer's way when he gets mad.

He doesn't say anything for so long that I squirm in front of him. There's no question he understands now that Damon suspects me of sleeping with Keith, but I can't say those words out loud.

"How bad is it?" he asks after way too long. "Tell me what's going on." He waves toward the closed door. "None of these people know, so you better talk to someone."

If I ever thought I could get away with keeping this to myself, those words shatter those hopes forever. He's right. I have to tell someone. I've kept this secret for way too long.

I wave my hands a few more times, but that doesn't help me get the words out, so I pace around the room instead. I knit my fingers together until my knuckles ache. I can't look at Keith or I really will crumble.

"It started.....you know....when we first started going out....he was just really jealous if I talked to another guy or even looked at another guy. Then he started accusing me of cheating on him, but now it's gotten so much worse."

"What happened to make it so much worse?" Keith demands. "Did something happen?"

"No, not like that. I guess he just finally put it together how close we all are here....." I wave toward the firehouse praying to Almighty God that Keith understands. I don't know if I can say any more.

He scowls even more darkly and then finally looks away. "Yeah. I guess that would make anyone suspicious....but that's no call for him to treat you like that. Did he do or say anything after you left yesterday?"

He hesitates for a split second and then notices the expression of stark, staring terror on my face. I couldn't tell Keith about what happened between me and Damon after we left yesterday.

"Don't answer that," he tells me. "In fact, don't say anything at all. I'll go see John...."

"NO!!" I clamp my mouth shut, but it's too late. Maybe everyone in the firehouse heard that. "Please don't tell anyone. It's bad enough that you know...."

"Screw that!" he snarls. "Everyone needs to know about this! If you two split up and he got together with someone else, he could wind up doing the same damn thing. You can't let that happen."

"Please don't tell John...or anyone else!" I take a step toward him and put out my hand. I realize a second too late that I was about to touch him.

Keith and I have always been close. Neither of us thought twice about touching each other on the job. I even saw him with his shirt off yesterday and it wasn't the first time.

He purses his lips and changes his tone. He sounds softer now, but no less determined. "I understand why you don't want anyone to know about this, but I have to tell John about Damon threatening me. You know I have to tell him that."

I can't control my hands anymore. They seem to have taken on a life of their own, but I can't come up with any words for what I'm feeling. I want to cry and scream and run away all at the same time.

Someone from the firehouse was bound to find out about me and Damon eventually. I just wish it hadn't been Keith. I could live with anyone but him knowing.

Now he has to tell John. How can I ever face John again after this?

I get so agitated that I forget for a split second that Keith is still here. He's standing right in front of me watching me writhe out of my skin from all this turmoil eating me up inside. How did I ever act so happy-go-lucky around the firehouse before this? Is that all gone, too?

He finally breaks the spell by murmuring, "Hey! Come here. It's gonna be okay. Everything is gonna be okay."

He takes one step toward me, and before I even think to stop it, he puts his arms around me and pulls me into a hug.

How many times have I hugged him without ever even realizing how much it meant? He's always been there. He's one of the people I value most on the crew.

He closes me in his big arms and then, like something out of a heavenly dream, he kisses me on the forehead.

"Everything is gonna be okay," he whispers again. "I promise."

I collapse into his arms. I don't see how anything will ever be okay after this, but if he's saying it, it must be true. He would never lie to me.

I fall against his chest. He's so much bigger than I am. Maybe he's even big enough to handle this. In fact, I know he is.

He finally pushes me back, rubs his hands up and down my arms, and then strokes my cheek and pushes a stray lock of hair out of my eyes.

He bends down and peers into my eyes at close range. "Are you gonna be okay? I can get John to give you the day off work if you need it."

"No...." I croak. "I want to work."

"Okay. No one else has to find out about this. I'll tell John and he'll keep it confidential. Okay?"

I nod, too distraught to speak. Just the simple fact that Keith knows somehow makes the whole catastrophe so much more real. Now I really feel how much Damon has destroyed my life. I tricked myself before about how bad it was.

Keith somehow senses that I'm too upset to function in this conversation any longer. He takes my arm, leads me out of the locker room, and pushes me toward the garage. The crew isn't in there anymore.

We get out onto the floor and hear everyone upstairs in the break room. "Go upstairs and go into the break room," Keith murmurs. "I'll go see John in his office. No one has to know."

I nod again and walk away. I can't look at him when I know what he's about to do.

Chapter 5: Keith

I knock on John's office door. It's ajar so I push it open. "Can I talk to you for a sec?" I ask.

He looks up from his computer. "Sure. Take a seat." He leans back in his chair to look at me. "What's up?"

I sit down opposite him and take a deep breath. Telling Leila I was going to talk to John about her and Damon—that was easy. Now I'm sitting here and I realize why she wanted to keep this all so quiet. I'm not sure I can go through with it.

I clamp my hands between my knees and look down at the floor. Why the hell am I so nervous? John is the one person I trust most in the world. If he can't handle this, no one can.

I used to think that about myself. I could probably handle it if it was anyone but her.

His eyebrows pinch in the middle and he frowns. "Is something wrong, man?"

"Yeah, something's wrong," I mutter and take another deep breath before I blurt out the whole damn thing. "After I talked to you yesterday....I was about to leave for the afternoon....and I heard Damon and Leila arguing in the alley behind the firehouse."

Now he really does frown. "Arguing! That isn't like them."

"Oh, it was way worse than an argument. I'm pretty sure he either slapped her or belted her right before I got there. I didn't see so I can't be certain, but when I did get there, he was yanking her around by the arm, threatening her, calling her a bunch of nasty names, and accusing her of......"

I break off. I can't tell John about Damon suspecting me of cheating with Leila. That would be going too far.

John's eyes go hard when I tell him about Damon smacking Leila. I'm the kind of guy most people wouldn't want to meet in a dark alley, but John is the guy that *I* wouldn't want to meet in a dark alley, especially when he looks like that.

He tightens his jaw and listens to me blunder through the rest. "He thinks......he thinks I'm screwing around with Leila behind his back. She says he's jealous of how close we all are on the crew....and then he threatened to put me down if I didn't back off."

He doesn't say anything for a minute. I can't remember a minute ever lasting so long. I really wish I could get out of this damn office, but I can't leave now—not until he tells me he's finished with me.

He glares at me for what seems like an eternity before he raises his eyebrows and leans forward. "Well! We definitely have to report that."

"She wants this all kept strictly confidential." I pass my hand across my eyes. "Sorry. I don't know why I said that."

"Of course it's confidential. I'll file a complaint with the Police Department and get Damon cited for malicious trespass so he won't be allowed to come onto firehouse property again. We can't have him coming around when Leila is on her shift if he's going to interfere with her work."

"Thanks, man," I mutter.

He glances up, but only for a second. He taps on his computer for a minute while I shift my weight in my seat. How long does he plan to keep me here?

He finally looks up, rests his elbows on the desk, and leans across it to confront me. "So....how is she?"

I shrug. I'm finding it nearly impossible to look at him. "You know....about like you'd expect.....she's a mess. All her spark is gone. I hate to think she's been playing an act with us all these years."

"I doubt that. If I had to guess, I'd say the Leila we've been seeing at the firehouse is the real Leila. The other one is something he created. It isn't really her."

My head shoots up. "You think?"

"I'd put money on it. I bet you anything you like this is the one place in the world where she feels like she can be herself. Don't take that away from her. Let her come out of her shell. Things might change, now that you and I know. Just give her the space to come back without pushing this in her face."

Now I really have to look away. Leila. I never realized until now how much I care about her. "Yeah, man. You're right."

"Go on and get out of here. I'll talk to you later."

I wander out of his office. The hall outside leads me straight past the break room where I hear everyone laughing, talking, and the hiss of someone cranking the top off a soda bottle.

Then I hear Leila laughing with the others. Her voice sounds smooth, casual, and light-hearted—the way she always sounds.

John is right. She's always felt comfortable at the firehouse. She's family to us all the same way we are to her.

She never hesitated to touch me until today. She didn't hesitate to check my back yesterday or to sit next to me. She didn't act even marginally uncomfortable about me grabbing her when Danny knocked us over or when I landed on top of her during the cave-in.

We've been doing things like that for years and it never became an issue until now. It never would have become an issue if Damon hadn't brought it up.

Now I can't stop thinking about her. Does he see something neither of us sees? Is there something between me and Leila? Could there ever be?

I didn't mean anything when I mentioned them breaking up....but what if?

She's beautiful, sweet, kind, professional—she's one of the best paramedics we've ever had *because* she's so kind and attentive.

I wouldn't have minded taking my shirt off for one of the other paramedics to check my back, but it meant something different when she did it.

I'm not saying it meant anything serious, but she's more than family—more than a sister or a friend. I can't explain it to myself—except that I can.

She's always been special to me and I know I'm special to her. We're as close as we can be without actually being involved.

Would I have ever gotten together with her if she hadn't gotten together with Damon? I knew her and worked with her before they got together. It just never crossed my mind to take it to the next level.

I can't explain that away by saying I didn't want to mess up our professional relationship. It went beyond that.

Maybe I just cared about her too much to go there. Our friendship was too important.

Even calling it friendship sounds like an insult. She's more than a friend—so what is she? I'm not even sure.

I can't go into the break room with the whole crew in there. I want Leila to have some time to herself before I see her again.

I could pound Damon's head in for spoiling this. He's cost me one of my closest relationships, and if he has his way, he'll cost her even more. What a chump.

I go back downstairs to the garage. It's deserted. I climb into the rescue truck's driver's seat and pull out the logbook for no particular reason.

I don't need to do anything or check anything, but I need to occupy myself with something at least outwardly work-related while I clear my head.

I flip the pages while I think. Without meaning to, I start to imagine what it would be like between me and Leila if she did break up with Damon. I shouldn't even be thinking that. If she broke up with him, it would take her one hell of a long time to get over it.

She might have to go through years of therapy to cope with her experience. She would need a friend during that time much more than just another man hanging around making her life complicated.

God Almighty, why am I even thinking about Leila that way? She's my coworker. I would risk the whole firehouse culture if I messed that up—to say nothing of my own career.

I really need to pull my head out of the clouds, but fortunately, right at that minute, the firehouse alarm goes off again. I don't even have to move from my seat except to dive into my turnouts. I'm the first one loaded into the truck because I'm already in it.

Now it's my turn to get some payback on Danny by telling him to hurry up. He doesn't have a bunch of medical supplies to use as an excuse.

The great news is that I don't have to turn around. I don't have to see Leila getting into the back before I open the garage doors and roll the truck outside.

"What's the address?" I yell to Billy over the siren's wail.

"Fourteen-eighty-two Cliffview Road!" he tells me. "It's a private residence! Dispatch says there's an old lady stuck in the attic."

I turn around and stare at him. "The attic? You're serious." Then I remember to watch the road.

"Hey—I'm just telling you what's in the call-out."

I concentrate on getting to the address, which is an old-fashioned farmhouse way out in the country. There's no one for miles around. I switch off the siren when we pull into the driveway. "I don't see any cars in the driveway."

Billy frowns at the notice from dispatch again. "This is weird. The call says it's an extrication—not medical."

"Maybe the old lady had a stroke and she's confused." Now I have to turn around. "Chris and Leila, you come with us. We might need you if the patient is injured or anything."

"You got it," Chris tells me.

I don't let myself look at Leila. This is shaping up to be the most uncomfortable call I've ever been on.

Danny, Billy, Caleb, and I head for the front porch. I stick my head inside. "Fire Department! We got a call that you needed help! Is anyone home?"

No one answers me. "Maybe the ghosts made the call," Danny surmises.

No one laughs. The house definitely has a spooky vibe with dust everywhere. The floorboards creak underfoot and my voice echoes up the stairs.

"The call said she's in the attic," Billy reminds me. "I guess we go up."

I head up the stairs and keep calling, "Hello?! Is anyone home? We're with the Fire Department! We're here to help!"

"Just make a low moaning noise if you can hear us," Danny murmurs, but I hear a quaver in his voice. This call is starting to freak all of us out.

Chris and Leila hang out in the back behind us guys. The house has three stories and I make it all the way to the top calling and calling and calling.

I go to the end of the hall where it ends at the master bedroom. I poke my head into every room. "Anybody here? Call out if you need help!"

I search the master bedroom. Nothing. I turn around. "We better go. I'll call dispatch and tell them we couldn't find....."

That's when I hear the faintest noise. I have to strain my ears to hear it.

"Hello?!" I yell. "Where are you?"

I hear the sound again, but it doesn't sound like a human voice. It really does sound like a ghost moaning.

Danny grabs my arm and hangs onto me. "Oh, no!" he whimpers. "They're after us!"

"Get the hell off me, you dope!" I shake him off and follow the sound back to the master bedroom. "It's coming from in here. HEL-LO!! Where are you? We're with the Fire Department!"

A very faint voice "Up here! Please help me!"

We spread out and search the master bedroom a second time until Billy calls, "Here! I found it!"

He leads the way into the master bedroom walk-in closet. It's huge—almost a bedroom in its own right. That's where we find the fold-out stairs leading to the attic.

We climb up and find an old lady sitting in a chair. She and the chair are the only things in the whole attic.

She sits in the very center of the empty attic staring at a tiny window overlooking the farmland outside. This is looking more and more like a scene out of a horror movie.

I inch over to her, and when I bend down to look into her eyes, she looks straight past me toward the window. Is she about to turn into a raving serial killer? I honestly wouldn't be surprised.

"Are you okay?" I ask. "The call said you were trapped up here."

"Please help me!" she sobs and her lips quiver, but she still doesn't make eye contact. "I'm stuck in here and I can't get down!"

"What's the problem?" Billy asks. "You look all right to me."

"She isn't all right," Leila cuts in and elbows us out of the way. "You can see she has an altered mental state. She may have suffered a cerebral event and can't see or can't find her way back to the stairs." She catches me looking at her. "You guys bring up the gurney from the ambulance. We can carry her down the stairs on this chair since she obviously can't walk on her own."

Billy and Danny leave together and I hear them downstairs laughing about the ghosts. I can't say I blame them.

Chris and Leila start working on the old lady. Leila takes the lady's blood pressure and Chris checks the patient's pupils. "You're right, Leila. Her left pupil is blown wide open."

"Her pressure is spiking," Leila replies. "She's got an intracranial bleed. We need to get her out of here."

Chris bends over her jump kit to open her drug box. Leila turns around to say something to me. At last, now that we're on a call together, we can just act professionally without a lot of awkward silences and tension between us.

Right at that moment, the old lady slumps in her chair. Her chin falls on her chest and she folds forward. She almost topples right onto Leila, but instinct takes over and I shoot out my arm to catch the old lady before she face-plants.

I wind up putting my arm straight over Leila's shoulder. She freezes in place staring at the old lady while we all reorient ourselves to the fact that the patient just passed out right in front of us.

Leila recovers and raises her arms to do something, but the old lady's body goes completely limp and slumps sideways away from my hand.

I jump forward and shoot out my other arm to stabilize her body. She weighs more than I expected, and before I think to correct, I'm standing there with my arms on either side of Leila to brace the old lady into position.

"Holy crap!" Leila whispers. "She's crashing on us! Lower her onto the floor, Keith."

She ducks out from between my arms, but not before I catch her making eye contact with me. This is nothing we haven't done a thousand times before. We've been in way more intimate contact than this and it didn't mean a thing.

It's all over in a fraction of a second. Leila stands up, grabs the old lady from the side, and we work together to lower the woman's body onto the floor just as I hear Billy and Danny coming back.

The metal gurney wheels clank down in the master bedroom walk-in closet. They're right downstairs. "Hey!" I yell over my shoulder. "The patient passed out! We need a backboard and all the extrication equipment up here!"

"What about a neck collar?" Danny asks. "Did she fall and get a head injury?"

"No, smartass! She didn't fall! You can skip the collar—and the attitude."

I hear them chuckle to each other. Then Danny leaves and Billy climbs up.

I have to step out of the way to give Chris and Leila enough space to work. They start putting in an IV and pumping the woman full of drugs. Then Leila intubates the patient and starts ventilating her with oxygen.

Finally, Danny returns with the backboard. Now it's mine and Billy's turn to step in, strap the old lady to the board, and we carry the woman downstairs to the ambulance where Naomi and Sophie take her off our hands.

Chris, Leila, Danny, Billy, Caleb, and I stand in the front yard and watch the ambulance drive away. We have no more reason to stay here, now that the patient is on her way to the hospital.

Leila turns to me. "Thanks for reacting so quickly. You saved her from getting a head injury for sure."

I try to shrug that away. "It was nothing."

She smiles at me and thank the stars it's her old warm friendly smile. She squeezes my shoulder in her old warm friendly way and walks back to the house to get her gear.

She's always thanking me for doing stuff like that. I don't need to read anything into it because it doesn't mean anything—except that we're back to being just friends. She doesn't think of me that way because she's already in a relationship with someone else.

Relief and gratitude sweep over me. I don't have to think about it that way anymore, either, thank Heaven. I supported her as a friend. That's all I need to do.

Chapter 6: Leila

I cross the pool hall to the far corner where the whole firehouse crew stands mobbed around four tables. Four different games are in progress while the rest of the crew socializes in the corner.

Food covers a standing bar along the pool hall's back wall and the waitress keeps bringing trays of drinks.

"And then a huge white ghost came sweeping down the stairs, opened its mouth, and tried to eat us all," Danny is saying.

The others laugh. "How did you survive?" Ellen Foreman asks.

I shouldn't think of her as Ellen Foreman anymore—not after she and John got married last month. I still find it hard to think of her as John's wife. She was my partner on the rescue truck for years. Now she doesn't even work for the fire crew anymore.

Billy steps in, hooks his arm around Danny's neck, and Billy's weight almost makes Danny's knees buckle. Billy towers six inches over Danny and weighs fifty pounds more.

"He threw himself into the ghost's mouth and saved us all," Billy tells Ellen. "That's the only reason we're standing here talking about it—thanks to this little cherub's sacrifice. May he rest in peace."

"I did not!" Danny throws an elbow into Billy's ribs and pushes him off. "Quit lying."

I pull up to take my place in the circle. "Tell them about how you saved the patient from falling on her face and getting a head injury," I tell Danny.

Keith snorts across the circle, but he doesn't interrupt. Danny turns bright red. "I'll save that one for my memoir."

"I'll bet you will," Keith rumbles. "That book will be a top fiction bestseller."

Everyone busts out laughing and I cast a glance around the pool hall. "This makes a nice change from the beach barbecues, doesn't it?"

"Just don't look too closely at the table on the far end," Chris tells me. "I sense impending disaster."

All eyes swivel to the last pool table in line where Ellis is playing against Jordan Markette, our newest paramedic hire. John and Andy are playing at the table next to them.

"Have you worked with Jordan yet, Leila?" Sophie asks me from across the circle.

"Not yet and it doesn't look like I'm going to get a chance to. It looks like he doesn't appreciate Ellis's sense of humor."

"Who are you kidding?" Keith growls. "Ellis is slaughtering him at the game. It looks to me like Jordan doesn't like to lose."

"He better toughen up if he wants to ride on this crew," Ellen observes.

"You said it, not me," Keith replies, and right then, the waitress comes back with a bunch of new drinks.

Everyone steps forward to collect their orders and I turn to the waitress to tell her what I want and to order for Damon. He's just getting off work so he isn't here yet.

I take off my jacket, and when I rejoin the circle, I wind up standing next to Keith. I don't think anything of it. Things have been easy between me and Keith ever since yesterday's call to the farmhouse.

Now we can finally go back to the way things were before—and they were so good before this whole Damon thing messed everything up.

Keith tips up his bottle of beer. He's definitely more relaxed since the farmhouse call, so maybe the ghosts did something for him.

A few minutes later, Ellis comes back—alone. "Where's Jordan?" Chris asks.

"He left," Ellis replies and picks up his beer glass from the standing bar.

"He left?!" Sophie demands. "Just like that? Did you say anything to offend him?"

"Not at all. I told him to come on over and join us. I told him everyone wants to talk to him and get to know him....and I told him he could play you next and wipe the floor with you to make up for me beating him."

Everyone bursts out laughing. Sophie blushes. "I'm not that bad."

"You're better than me," I tell her.

"That isn't saying much," Keith counters. "You need your eyes checked or something."

"Hey! Watch it!" I yell, but I can't help joining in the laughter. My pool playing is the stuff of legend around the firehouse—and not in a good way. Keith is right. I'm useless.

"So tell us, Leila," Ellis chimes in. "Tell us what the ghost of Cliffview Road really looked like."

"Not that stupid ghost again!" Keith groans. "Can't we come up with anything else to talk about?"

"We could talk about who's going to clean out the break room fridge," Danny suggests. "I don't think anyone has cleaned it since the late Depression Era."

I turn to Keith and bump my knuckles against his elbow. "Hey, tell everyone about how Danny held onto your arm and hid behind you for protection from the ghosts."

The whole circle explodes and I definitely catch Keith grinning at me. I grin back. Now we're getting somewhere. Keith is too nice to use that little piece of ammunition against his brother.

Just then, Damon comes over to me, puts his arm around my waist from behind, and kisses me on the cheek.

"Hey, Damon! You made it!" Danny calls. "The waitress should be coming back with your drinks any second now."

"I ordered for you," I tell Damon. "I hope you don't mind."

"I don't mind at all. Hi, everybody." He turns to me. "Do you mind if I talk to you for a second?"

He steers me away from the group and stops me by one of the other tables—a table far enough away so no one can overhear us.

"Did you have a good day?" I ask. "How did your shift go?"

"Don't give me that shit!" he snaps in an undertone. "I just saw you making eyes at Keith again."

"Making eyes! I wasn't making eyes at him. We were joking about a call we went on yesterday."

"Spare me your pathetic excuses. I know what I saw. Now go get your jacket. We're leaving."

"I don't want to leave!" I exclaim. "We just got here and I wasn't doing anything. I work with Keith. I have to talk to him. There's nothing suspicious about that."

"You were doing a lot more than talking to him. I saw you flirting with him with my own eyes."

I open my mouth to argue back. Don't ask me why. I already know it won't do any good.

Before I can say anything, he lunges for me, grabs my arm, and twists it hard enough to make me cry out in pain. "I told you to go get your jacket. Don't give me any static or you'll be sorry."

"Let go of me, Damon!" I fire back and realize too late that I forgot to keep my voice down.

He wrenches my arm nearly out of its socket, but right then, a deep, rumbly voice booms out through the noise of the pool hall. "Is there a problem here?"

Damon and I both spin around to see Keith, Billy, Danny, Ellis, and Caleb all standing there watching us. Keith occupies the position in the very middle of the group. He must have been the one to bring the other guys over here to confront Damon.

Damon doesn't even notice the others. He narrows his eyes at Keith. "You better get the hell out of here and go back to your table if you know what's good for you. You've done enough damage already."

"Is that so? What exactly did I do?" Keith waves at the rest of the group. "Go on. Announce your personal business to the world. I was prepared to keep your little problem confidential, but now you've come in here pushing one of my colleagues around, so now everybody knows. Go on and tell them what I did. I'm waiting."

Damon hesitates while he glares at Keith. Damon can spout all his delusional nonsense when he and I are alone together. Does he really have the balls to broadcast it to the whole fire crew?

"You know what you did," he finally snarls. "You've been coming between me and Leila since the beginning."

Keith snorts in his face. "You really are a lunatic, aren't you? If Leila wanted me, she would have gone with me in the first place. She wouldn't have wasted the last year of her life with a lowlife like you."

Damon steps right up to Keith and gets in his face. Damon's chest bumps into Keith's chest, which only makes Damon look ridiculous because Damon bounces off a solid wall of muscle. Keith doesn't budge.

"You better get the hell out of my way," Damon hisses. "Leila and I are leaving."

"She is never going anywhere with you ever again, you piece of shit," Keith growls just as low. "Lay a finger on her and you'll be looking at all of us, not just one woman half your size."

Damon clenches his fists at his sides and I brace myself for a pool hall brawl to break out, but right then, the group of men breaks apart and John pushes his way between them.

He plants himself next to Keith and looks down his nose at Damon even though he and John are the same height. "You aren't welcome at firehouse functions anymore, Damon," John tells him.

Damon snorts. "As if I would want to hang out with a bunch of dumbass firefighters."

"Maybe you don't, but Leila does, and if she does, she'll come alone. We protect our own, Damon. If we find out you're making Leila's life difficult, we won't hesitate to intervene."

"Is that some kind of threat?" Damon fires back. "Does that mean you'll all come around to my house and kick my ass? I can call in a couple dozen cops to put all of you in the ground."

"I'm sure you won't be able to call in a couple dozen cops to protect you when they find out why we're after you," John replies. "Besides, I'm sure we can come up with other ways to put the screws to you. I'm pretty good friends with Jim Walker, you know. One of him can take on your couple dozen cops any day of the week. Now get the hell out of here.....and Leila will be staying here."

Damon glares at him....and then Damon's gaze slides sideways to the other firefighters standing around. He seems to get the picture that he's one guy against all of them—and that's not counting the Chief of

Police. None of Damon's cop buddies will be stepping out of line to cover his back.

He clenches his fists again and then storms out of the pool hall without turning around to look at me. I collapse onto the nearest barstool and cradle my head in my hand. That went about as badly as I could possibly have feared it would.

Now everyone knows about me and Damon—and about Damon suspecting Keith of messing around with me. Now what am I gonna do?

Before I can decide, the crew gathers around me all talking at once. The women pat me on the back and ask me if I'm okay. Ellen offers to check my arm, but I shrug that away. "I'm all right," I murmur.

"What a jerk!" Sophie exclaims. "How long has he been acting like this?"

"Well….he was always jealous, but it's gotten a lot worse lately."

"You really need to give him the boot," Chris tells me. "You don't need that crap."

"Leave her alone," Ellen interjects. "It isn't for us to say what she should do with her relationship."

"Chris is right," Naomi adds. "You can do so much better."

I look up and find them all surrounding me—my friends, my coworkers—my firehouse family.

"You heard what Keith said," Naomi adds. "You should have gotten with him first and skipped this whole Damon thing."

"Yeah, Keith is a prince," Chris adds, "and he obviously loves you."

"Chris!" Sophie gasps. "He doesn't love her!"

"You know what I mean!" Chris counters. "He admires and respects her. He always has. Everybody knows it." She turns back to me. "You know it's true. When some woman does bag Keith Brewer, she's going to be one hell of a lucky woman."

"No one is going to bag Keith," Ellen interjects again. "You make him sound like some kind of prey animal."

The others laugh and then they all start talking about the guys on the firehouse crew. They're all single except for John.

Chris, Sophie, and Naomi start comparing the guys and their looks and personalities. I glance over at the guys, who are all talking in their own little huddle. Are they comparing which of us is the best-looking and has the nicest personality?

Then I spot John and Keith standing off to one side away from everyone else. What are they talking about? Is John asking Keith if he and I are together?

If Keith mentioned that, does that mean he's thinking about it? Does that mean he's thinking of me in that way? Should I be concerned about that?

Chapter 7: Leila

Chris and Sophie walk me out to my car where we stand around laughing some more about Danny's ghost. "That call is going down in firehouse history," Sophie tells me. "I really wish I could have been there."

"It wasn't that spectacular at the time," I tell them. "It has definitely gotten better with age."

Chris steps forward to hug me. "I better go. I'll see you both tomorrow."

I kiss her on the cheek. "Thanks for your support tonight. I couldn't have done it without all of you."

"You bet," she tells me. "Call me if you need anything."

She walks off to her car. "I better go, too," Sophie tells me. "I was supposed to call my parents tonight, so I can just imagine the mountain of frantic texts that will be waiting for me when I get home."

I laugh. "Good luck with that. See you tomorrow."

She leaves, too, and I turn to unlock my car. The world feels emptier without the crew in it and now I'm on my way home to spend the night alone.

I really need to decide what to do about Damon. Everyone on the fire crew that is brave enough to offer a suggestion thinks I should dump him and they're probably right.

I just don't want to admit defeat. That's the problem. I don't want to admit that I failed at another relationship.

I should have seen the warning signs. I should have made an early exit when I saw Damon acting jealous early on. Then I wouldn't be in this situation now.

I don't want to break up with him, but maybe all these women are right that I can do so much better. What if Keith really is thinking of me that way?

Even if he isn't, he might be. Someone as good as he is might be thinking of me that way…or might think of me that way in the future. I shouldn't see myself as trapped with Damon when I'm not.

I drive back to my house. I'm tired from staying out so late and I need to get up early tomorrow morning to do it all again.

I chuckle again when I think about Danny's ghost. He seems to be milking the story for all its worth even though he's the butt of his own jokes. He's good that way. He can take a joke and roll with it.

I pull my car into the driveway, switch off the engine, and take my handbag up to the house. I'm selecting my front door key from my keychain when Damon steps out of the bushes.

I jump and my hand flies to my heart. "Damon! You scared me."

He saunters toward me really slowly across the porch. "You should be scared after the crap you pulled at the pool hall."

"I didn't pull anything at the pool hall." I turn back to the door. "You're imagining things, but the rest of the crew didn't. You should have kept it in private. Now everyone knows about it and John sure won't forget it."

"He's a waste of space, that guy," Damon snaps.

I spin around a second time and stare at him. This idiot really must be living in a fantasy world if he said something like that about John

Brewer. Everyone in town admires John. He's a legend and rightfully s o.

That's the moment when my mind snaps. I don't need to reason with Damon. I don't even need to be having this conversation with him. I don't need Damon for anything at all. I would be better off alone than spending even one more minute with him.

"I have to work tomorrow," I tell him. "I'm tired and I want to go to sleep. I'll see you later."

"I'm talking to you!" He lunges for me and grabs my arm again. It hurts, but I'm all finished playing games, and for the first time ever, I'm not scared of him.

"We aren't talking about anything ever again!" I spit back and yank my arm out of his grip. "We're finished. You made a fool of yourself at the pool hall earlier. You've been cited for malicious trespass on the firehouse grounds and banned from firehouse functions. I never have to see you or talk to you again. So you can go home and leave me alone. We're finished."

"We aren't anywhere near finished until I say we are." He makes another dive to grab my arm. That's his favorite trick.

I wait just long enough for him to clamp his fingers around my arm. Then I spin around and stab my keys into the back of his knuckles as hard as I can.

He roars in pain and yanks his hand away real fast. "You bitch! What was that for?"

I dart several steps backward to get away from him. "We're finished, Damon! Do you got that? We're over—done! I never want to see you again. Get off my property and don't come near me again! Is that clear enough for you to understand? We aren't together anymore. Keep away from me!"

He plants himself right there in front of my door and puts his hands on his hips. "What are you going to do to make me? Huh? You better come here and apologize real nice if you want to set foot in this house ever again."

I stare at him, but he doesn't move. He really means it. He'll block me from entering my own house rather than accept that I'm breaking up with him.

I don't have time for this and I sure as hell won't stand out here all night waiting for him to leave.

I turn on my heel and walk back to my car. Thank God I didn't lock the door and I already have my keys in my hand. I get behind the wheel, fire up the engine, and drive away with him still standing there.

Don't ask me where I'm going to stay tonight. I could call any of my fellow paramedics from the fire crew. They'd be happy to let me stay at their houses. I could even call John and Ellen. They would let me stay with them and Oakleigh, but I don't want to impose on them.

I make up my mind and drive to the firehouse. It's late, so everyone from the night crew is already asleep in the bunk room upstairs. I have to be back here for work in a few hours anyway, so why not?

I stretch out fully clothed on an empty bunk and shut my eyes. I'm safe here. Damon won't come after me here. If worse comes to the worst, I can always stay here until this whole thing blows over. I'm sure John won't mind.

For once in my life, I don't feel ashamed about the rest of the crew finding out about tonight. They all said I should dump Damon and I did. If he can't accept it, that's his problem, not mine.

I relax and start to drift off to sleep. Poor Damon. He's probably too dim to realize that neither Keith nor I would ever have thought about each other like that if Damon hadn't started accusing us of sneaking around behind his back.

Now I'm single again and I'm definitely thinking about Keith now. If I ever get with someone else, Keith Brewer is exactly the kind of man I would want to get with.

He's always been supportive, kind, friendly, and he's always been a perfect gentleman toward me. What's not to like about that?

Chapter 8: Keith

I put my duffel bag in my locker and take out my jacket. I have another few hours to kill before it's time to go home and get some shut-eye for tomorrow's shift.

I shut my locker door, turn around, and stop dead in my tracks when I find John standing there. He squares his shoulders at me in a very big-brotherly way.

I stiffen at the sight. "Can I help you?" I ask and hope I sound steadier than I feel. I've never had this many confrontations with John in such a short space of time.

"I have to ask—for the sake of the whole crew," he begins. "Tell me straight. Is there anything going on between you and Leila—really? Is there any truth to Damon's suspicions?"

"No way!" I exclaim. "Never! I swear it! I would never....."

"I just wondered after your comments at the pool hall...."

"NO!!" I practically yell. "Never! I never....ever......"

He nods. "Okay, man. I believe you."

"I love her....like a sister, I mean...." God, I sound like a dope! "She's great, but I would never mess with the firehouse like that.....although, I gotta tell you the truth—I've been thinking about it since he mentioned it. I never thought about it before he brought it up. I would never go there!"

He nods again. "All right. I just wondered. I believe you."

"Is that it?" I ask. "Is that all you wanted to know?"

"Yep. If you tell me nothing is going on between you and Leila, I believe you."

"Well, it isn't."

He just keeps nodding. "Okay. See you around."

He walks out and leaves me shaking. I have to remind myself more than once that he wouldn't say he believes me if he didn't. John doesn't do that. I'm okay. I'm in the clear.

I can't get out of the firehouse fast enough. I get into my truck and drive back to my apartment, but I can't keep still. I take a shower and change my clothes, but I'm suffering from a serious case of cabin fever.

I can't remember ever feeling this jumpy. This whole Leila situation is really getting to me. Just when I think I'm on top of it, something else comes along and shatters my world.

I can't decide what to do about that, so I get in my car and drive around town for a while.

I end up driving down Cliffview Road and get a nice chuckle when I pass the haunted farmhouse—except that it isn't haunted—not now. Two cars sit in the driveway and light streams through the living room windows. I hope the old lady got some relatives to come and stay with her.

I head back into town and drive around aimlessly for a while. I stop at a stoplight and hear dance music coming through my rolled-down window from a club across the intersection.

A bunch of people stand outside in a line waiting to get in, but the bouncer seems to be letting everybody through.

I park and go over there, show him my ID, and step inside. Flashing colored strobe lights glance across the dance floor. Couples and single people gyrate out there and on the balcony overlooking the floor.

I shoulder my way to the bar and get a beer, but the music is too loud here. I see people sitting at tables on a different mezzanine and there's another bar up there.

I climb upstairs and sit down at the bar where I can look over the railing at the dance floor. There are a lot of beautiful girls here. Maybe I'll pick one of them up. I have nothing to lose. I'm a free agent with nothing better to do.

I take another sip from my glass and turn back to people-watching when I see four women at a table in the corner. It's in the very back of the mezzanine away from everyone else.

The four women have their heads together talking, and right then, the one nearest the outside with her back to me turns around. It's Leila. I don't recognize the other three women with her.

The other three look at me at the same time and then they all go back to talking to each other like schoolgirls on the playground.

I get a flash of what I must look like to them. I'm wearing a white T-shirt, a leather bomber jacket, blue jeans, and tan leather work boots. Everyone at the firehouse is always teasing me about looking like a biker. I couldn't look more like one now unless I was actually sitting on a bike.

Leila doesn't turn around again, so I guess she's too busy talking to her friends. I can appreciate that. She didn't come here to see me any more than I came here to see her, so I turn back to my beer.

I'm just swiveling the other way to go back to watching the dancers when Leila breaks away from her table, whispers a few more things to her companions, and strolls right over to my stool.

She wears skin-hugging tight leggings that show off every curve, black pumps, and a nice black leather jacket, but hers is smaller and tighter than mine. Hers makes her look elegant, but not so flashy that she looks like she's out cruising to hook up with anyone.

Her outfit makes her look incredible, but she doesn't go all out with the body-contouring pencil dresses most of the women on the dancefloor wear. Leila really does look like she's just here to have a good time with her friends, not to see and be seen by all the guys who are on the hunt downstairs.

She wears her hair pulled up in a messy bun on top of her head with curling side wisps surrounding her angelic face. She looks so different like this than what I'm used to seeing at the firehouse, but she's still the beautiful, charming woman I know so well.

She sets down her drink next, sits on the stool next to mine, and smiles at me. "Hi."

"Hello," I reply. "You didn't have to come over here to talk to me. You're out with your friends. Aren't they offended that you ditched them to spend time with a troll like me?"

She laughs, blushes, and dips her eyelids. She really is beautiful. "I'd rather talk to you. You're more interesting."

I raise my eyebrows. "No one has ever called me that before."

"Well, you are....and I like talking to you better. We have more in common than I have with them."

"Who are they?" I glance over at the table. The other three women are still talking about and watching me and Leila. "I don't recognize them."

She waves them away without looking at them. "Just some people I know from school. We hang out every now and then—nothing serious."

"Won't Damon get jealous if you hang out with someone other than him—and let's not get started on how he'll react if he finds out you ditched your friends to talk to me. We don't want to create another nightmare for you to deal with."

She rolls her eyes, but she won't stop smiling. "Damon is always going to be a nightmare, and if he gets jealous, that's his problem. I dumped him yesterday, so he won't ever have anything to say about what I do ever again."

Now I really raise my eyebrows. "You dumped him? No way. I didn't expect that."

"What—you thought I would stay with him forever and keep putting up with his BS? I do have some self-respect left."

"That's great. I'm proud of you. I didn't realize....." I trail off. I don't want to make it sound like I thought she was too much of a doormat to kick Damon where he deserved to be kicked.

Just about any way I can think of to end that sentence sounds worse than the last, so I don't finish it.

"Anyway, it's over, so I can go out and enjoy myself if I want to....and I filed for a restraining order. He showed up at my house after I went home from the pool hall. I told him we were over and never to come near me again. Then he actually tried to block me from entering my own house, so the next day, I went downtown and filed for the order."

"Wow, what a child."

She laughs again. "So what about you?"

"What about me? You know me. My life doesn't get more exciting than hanging out with my family and working."

"Yeah." She beams at me. "I know."

"So I won't be too surprised if you decide I'm not interesting enough for you to talk to. You could be down there with all the beautiful people." I jerk my thumb toward the dance floor.

"I don't think so." She turns back to me, but right then, her three friends get up and *they* go downstairs to the dance floor. They start dancing with a bunch of guys who are obviously here to hook up with someone.

"There you go," I remark. "You missed the bus. Now you're stuck with me."

She bursts into another grin. "I'd rather be stuck with you than them."

I frown at her. "What's going on with you? Why do you keep dropping these comments about how interesting I am and how you'd rather spend time with me? You know I'm not interesting and you could find someone a lot better to spend time with."

Her smile slips, but only slightly. "I guess I just keep thinking about what you said at the pool hall—about how I could have been going out with you all this time instead of Damon."

I freeze to my chair. We are not having this conversation. "What about it?"

"I never thought about it before he mentioned it. I mean, I always thought people from the firehouse were off limits, you know. I thought it would be better not to foul the nest, so to speak. Then, after he started making accusations against you and you said at the pool hall that I could have been with you all along….it just made me think…..maybe……"

Her eyes shine even brighter…..or maybe I'm just noticing them for the first time. She's sitting awfully close on the next stool.

I glance down at her mouth. I only said that at the pool hall to point out what a moron Damon is, but I guess it's true. If I ever thought for an instant that Leila was available to me, I would have moved Heaven and Earth for a chance with her.

I just never thought she *was* available to me. I thought the same way she did, that she was off the list. Now I know for certain she's thinking the same thing.

I don't give myself a second to hesitate. I lean in and kiss her and she kisses me back—just for a second. I make it a quick, casual peck and then straighten up.

She gazes deeply into my eyes from just a few feet away, but I see all the same questions churning in her head. Are we really going there?

She doesn't react right away, so maybe I read too much into it.

"We probably shouldn't," I tell her. "We still have to work together."

"Right," she agrees. "We don't want to make the whole crew uncomfortable."

"Or ourselves," I add. "John asked me if there was anything going on between us and I told him there wasn't. We should probably keep it that way."

She nods. "Definitely."

That settles it, so we both turn back to the bar and drink our drinks. Now I really want to get out of here. I shouldn't have come and I shouldn't have kissed her, but at least we can put it behind us and get back to work.

"Do you ever think about rising in rank?" she asks. "Do you ever think about moving up the ladder and maybe becoming a fire chief yourself?"

I glance over and find her facing the bar on her stool the same way I am. We sit side by side both facing in the same direction, so I guess she's just passing casual conversation now.

"Not really," I reply. "I never thought about it. Why do you ask?"

"I just wondered. You're the highest-ranked firefighter on our crew. You've gone as far as you can go while still being John's subordinate. If you rose any higher, you would become a chief yourself and get your own firehouse somewhere."

"Maybe that's why I don't do it. Maybe I don't want my own firehouse."

She glances in my direction and smiles at me, but it's a friendly smile. It doesn't mean anything. "I know what you mean. I wouldn't want to leave Howe, either. The firehouse is something special. I should probably go home."

"I'll walk you out." I stand up, down the rest of my beer, and leave a tip on the bar before we both head for the stairs.

She scans the dance floor, but I don't see her friends anywhere. They've vanished into the crowd of other partiers.

I push forward to escort Leila through the crowd blocking the door. She shrinks closer to me and I get another surge of protective rage for her.

I've always felt protective toward her, but this is different. I don't want to protect her because she's special to me. I don't just want to protect her because she's my coworker and I don't just want to protect her from Damon.

I want to protect her because she's mine—or I want her to be mine. I don't want anyone coming near her—ever. I want to protect her because I want to be the man that protects her from everyone and everything.

I want her to shrink nearer to me because she wants me to protect her. I want her to feel that way toward me—that I'm the man in her life that she can come to for protection against everything.

We burst through the crowd into the cool night air and I walk her to the parking lot. I have to resist the urge to take her hand, but I definitely want to. I want us to be out in town together. I want us to go home together. I want us to do everything together—literally everything.

To hell with it. Wasn't I just thinking I would jump at the chance to make something happen between us? Why shouldn't I?

I shouldn't because she just broke up with an abusive asshole who treated her like dirt. I shouldn't because she probably needs time to recover from that. She needs time to get her head straight before she jumps into another relationship.

I shouldn't because we just agreed upstairs not to go there—for ourselves and for the good of the firehouse. She probably doesn't want to go back on that decision, now that we both made it, and she's right.

All those considerations outweigh my desire to take this further, but boy, I sure do want to. I want to take her home with me right now and keep her there forever.

I want to flatten anyone who comes near her, especially that twit Damon. I want to be the one he runs into every time he tries to insert himself into her life. I can just imagine how that would go.

We get to the parking lot and I walk her to her car. She takes out her keys and rifles through them until she finds to the right one.

She stops by the driver's door and smiles up at me. "It was really nice seeing you tonight—much more interesting than hanging out with those girls."

I make a face. "I doubt that."

She only grins more widely. "You're too humble for your own good."

"I doubt that, too. I wouldn't want to get a huge, swollen head like Danny's."

She laughs. "Well, good night. I guess I'll see you tomorrow at work."

"Yeah. Drive safely. Call me if you need anything."

"Thanks." She takes a step toward me, lays her hand on my arm, and kisses me on the cheek before she steps away.

I shouldn't read anything into that and I don't. It's the most friend-zone kiss ever, but at the exact moment when she pulls back, I catch her looking at me and I know.

She wants more, too. She just said all that upstairs because she thought she was supposed to. She wanted to give me an out the same way I wanted to give her an out, but she wants it. She wants it bad.

I don't remember the moment when it happened, but the next second, we're kissing like our lives depend on it. I crush her in my arms and devour her mouth for all I'm worth. I need to experience every particle of her right this minute. I don't want to wait a second longer.

She gasps for breath and her smell explodes in my nose. I grab the back of her hair and steer her mouth into mine, but she's kissing me just as fast and just as ravenously.

Her hands fly to my sides under my jacket and I feel her touching me through my T-shirt. She slides her hands up my ribs and a torch of fire goes through me. I need her. I need her right now.

I pivot her toward the car and smash her against the side while I drive my body into her. Every sensation rockets me out of my mind. I would take her right here in the parking lot, but that seems a little crude considering we've never even kissed before tonight.

She screws her arms out from under me, wraps them around my neck, and then her fingers thread into my hair while she claws at every part of me. She really wants this. She wants it as much as I do.

I flex my knees and drill my hips into her to make her squeal. Her body trembles all over and then she moans when I ease off and push in a second time.

She raises one knee and it grazes the outside of my leg. I could get between her thighs right now, but the very excitement of this moment somehow brings me back to my senses.

This isn't just some chick I picked up on the dance floor. This is Leila, my friend and colleague. I can't treat her like a disposable club conquest I'll never see again.

I'm going to see her again tomorrow morning when both of us are wearing our uniforms and facing a day of working together. I'll still need to be able to look this woman in the eye when that happens.

I'll still need to look the rest of the crew in the eye, too—including my brothers. The whole crew adores Leila. They wouldn't stand me disrespecting her—as if I would ever do that.

I ease off.....just a little.....just enough for both of us to cool down, but she doesn't let go of me. She presses her breasts into my chest and she won't stop kissing me even when I try to pull away.

I have to force myself to break her grip. I lay my hand against her cheek and let the power die, but my desire for her doesn't go away.

It will never go away. I want her. The horse has left the barn, and if it never happens between us, I'll always think of what might have been.

She runs her fingers through my hair and beard. I love the way she feels when she touches me.....and then, when she finally unwinds her arms from my neck and stands back, she slips one arm around my waist under my jacket.

She feels so delicate and beautiful. Everything about her captivates me, but tonight is over for me. I won't let it go any further. I can't.

I steal a few more kisses, but I have to slow myself down. Each of those kisses could pull me back into a whirlwind that would only end one way. I can't let that happen.

I finally straighten up, comb a few stray pieces of hair out of her eyes, and move back just a little more to put some space between us. "I should go," I murmur.

"Yeah," she whispers. "Have a good night."

"You, too." I can't help but kiss her one more time. "I'll see you tomorrow."

She smiles ever so slightly and turns away. "Night."

"Bye." I step away from her car and she gets behind the wheel.

I back off while she puts on her seatbelt and turns the ignition. Visions of kissing her swim in my head as she reverses and then drives out of the parking lot. I will definitely be dreaming about her tonight.

Chapter 9: Leila

I park my car in the staff lot behind the firehouse and take a minute to compose myself. I keep getting heart palpitations when I think about kissing Keith outside the club.

Now I'm going inside to have my first shift with him since it happened. I can just imagine how awkward things are going to get, but I have to bite the bullet. I can't let this spoil the fire crew for both of us and the rest of the crew, too.

I take another deep breath, get out of the car, and hang my duffel bag over my shoulder. I'm doing this. I have to do it. I have a full day of work in front of me and Keith is part of that.

I walk in through the garage doors. No one is around and I hear everyone talking up in the break room.

I put my stuff in my locker, but I can't spend the whole shift down here hiding by myself. I climb the stairs and walk into the break room.

Keith and Danny stand by the fridge talking about something. Ellis, Billy, Caleb, Andy, and Jordan sit at the table playing cards.

Sophie, Naomi, Brooke Elsworth, and Jessie Nash sit on the couches, two to a couch. They're all talking to each other. Chris sits alone on the loveseat while she taps on her phone.

"Hey, Leila's here!" Ellis calls out as soon as I walk in.

"Hey, Leila!" Andy yells over his shoulder. "John wants to talk to you about the next paramedic professional development course coming up. He said for you to go see him as soon as you got in."

"But not now," Caleb corrects. "He's out of the firehouse on city business, so you'll have to wait until he gets back."

"Oh, okay." I sit down next to Chris. "So are the rest of you going on the course, too?"

Chris puts her phone down. "He was just in here giving us the lowdown on it. What's going on with you? Did the excrement collide with the rotating device after you left the pool hall the other night? Damon sure looked steamed about John banning him from firehouse functions."

"Yeah, I'm pretty sure the rotating device suffered a fatal blow. I dumped him."

"No way!" She practically bounces off the couch and raises her hand to give me a high-five. "You go, girl! I'm so proud of you!"

I blush and try to shrug it away, but all the guys are already turning around to join the conversation. The other four paramedics leave their couches to gather around. Even Danny comes over to pat me on the back.

"How did he take it?" Naomi asks.

"Did you cut him off at the knees?" Caleb asks. "Please tell me you did."

I laugh nervously. "I just told him we're finished. That's all."

"Did he lose his shit completely?" Andy rubs his hands with glee. "I wish I could have been there to see his reaction."

"At least you won't have to put up with him interfering with your social life," Billy adds.

"Or making stupid accusations." Danny glances over his shoulder and notices Keith still standing apart by the fridge. He doesn't come over to get involved. "What's wrong with you? Aren't you going to at least congratulate her on dumping that idiot?"

"I already knew about it," Keith replies. "I bumped into Leila in town last night and she told me then. I already congratulated her."

Danny turns to face me and the rest of them start firing questions and comments at me like Keith isn't even there. None of them thinks anything of his statement and why should they? Everything he said was true. He just didn't mention the part about us making out.

I start telling them about Damon blocking me from going into my house and about spending the night at the firehouse and filing for the restraining order, but before I get through the story, we get another call.

The fire alarm interrupts me and we all race downstairs to the trucks. Chris and I hop into our seats and the rescue truck pulls out of the garage.

Keith and Billy yell back and forth about the address while Chris and I make some final checks on our gear.

I unzip the jump kit. "This is the jump kit from the ladder truck!" I yell over the siren. "What are they using?"

"No idea!" she yells back. "Maybe we'll have to toss it back and forth between both crews."

She smirks at her own joke and I laugh. "I guess I can ask John about it when he fills me in on the professional development course."

"Oh, look! There he goes!" She points out the window just as John drives past us going the other way. He sticks his arm out the window to wave at us and Keith waves through the rescue truck driver's window.

The next minute, the truck and ambulance pull into the parking lot of an apartment complex where the manager meets us. He tells us that our patient left a pan of steaks on the stove and fell asleep in his lounge chair with the burner still turned on.

Smoke billows from the third-floor window and the guys put on their oxygen tanks and masks before they go in to check the scene.

Chris and I suit up and follow them inside. A thick layer of black smoke fills the apartment with another layer of cleaner air three feet off the floor.

We find the patient lying sprawled in the living room with soot around his mouth—which means he passed out from smoke inhalation.

Chris gets busy fitting him with an oxygen mask while I take his vital signs. "His pulse oxygen concentration is 70%!" I yell through the mask.

I turn around to tell the guys to bring up a gurney so we can transport the patient to the hospital, but before I can say anything, Keith comes over to us wheeling the gurney from the ambulance.

He parks it by the patient and drops on one knee next to me. "Let's get him loaded up and out of this smoke. The ambulance is waiting right at the bottom of the stairs.

Billy and Danny come over to help and Chris and I back off while the guys hoist the patient onto the gurney. We transfer him to the ambulance and Brooke and Naomi drive off with him.

I pull off my oxygen mask and gasp in a lungful of fresh air. The guys, Chris, and I take our gear back to the rescue truck. Danny starts singing, "And another one bites the dust!"

"That is just crude," Keith tells him. "He didn't bite the dust. He's gonna be just fine."

"I meant he bit the dust before we got here," Danny corrects. "Can you imagine him falling on his face and crawling toward the stove before he passed out?"

"That isn't funny, Danny," I tell him. "The guy could have died."

"Don't pay any attention to this clown," Keith rumbles. "He was born without a conscience."

Danny gasps, but he won't stop grinning. "Ouch!" Then he brightens up. "But hey, at least I got the looks in the family. You can have the conscience as long as I don't grow up to look like you."

"You will never grow up," Keith growls.

"What about John?" Chris asks. "He got his share of the looks."

Danny pretends to scowl at her. "You did not just suggest that John is better-looking than me."

"I don't know," she counters. "He could definitely give you some competition. The guy is stunning."

Danny throws up his hands and spins away. "That's it. I quit. I'm not playing anymore."

He stalks off toward the rescue truck and the rest of us laugh at him behind his back. I pat Keith on the shoulder. "Don't worry. Conscience trumps good looks any day of the week."

He colors and turns away, but I catch him smiling anyway. We load into the trucks and head back to the firehouse, but the rest of the day passes normally. I don't sense any of the awkward tension I was dreading between me and Keith.

No one on the crew notices anything out of the ordinary because there is nothing out of the ordinary going on between us. Keith and I act the way we always have. Today is turning out to be one of the best days I can remember.

We go out on another medical call that goes just as smoothly. The rest of the time, the crew hangs out in the break room talking and joking the way we usually do.

John comes in at one o'clock and I go see him in his office to talk about the professional development course. "And we should replace the jump kit that we lost on the Forsyth Bank call," I tell him.

"I already ordered the stuff," he replies. "You can keep using the kit from the ladder truck in the meantime."

"What will the ladder truck crew use?"

"The rescue truck goes on more calls. The bag for the new jump kit will be here tomorrow and you can supply it from the stores we already have. Anything extra will come in with our next supply order."

"Wow! Great!" I exclaim. "That was so much easier than I expected. We all thought you would soil your trousers over the expense."

He laughs. "I would never blink at an expense where your jobs are concerned." He leans back in his chair and looks up at me. "I hear you and Damon are through. Congratulations."

"Thanks. I have a restraining order, so he shouldn't come around the firehouse anymore."

"Excellent. Good thinking. Hey, do me a favor and email me a copy of the order so I can send it to Jim Walker. He should know about this."

"Okay." I pull out my phone. "Sent."

"Perfect. See you later."

I leave his office feeling so much better about everything. This doesn't have to be a nightmarish grind like I thought.

I go downstairs to the locker room with the rest of the crew when it's time to clock out. "Naomi and I are going to a poetry slam tonight," Brooke tells me. "You should come."

Ellis falls on one knee in front of me, clasps his hands, and bats his eyelashes at me. "Shall I compare thee to a summer's day.....?"

"Plagiarism!" Keith yells across the locker room.

"The whole point of the slam is that you make everything up on the spot," Brooke tells Ellis. "You would get kicked out if you used that."

"Yeah, come up with something original and I might be impressed," I chime in.

Ellis gets to his feet and rubs his chin. "Hmm. I might be out of luck, then. I don't do poetry."

"I would be worried if you did," Keith growls and everyone laughs.

I turn back to my locker. "So what do you say?" Brooke asks again. "Do you want to come?"

"Um...maybe later. Text me the time and place."

"What do you have to do instead?" Naomi asks. "Don't tell me you have another guy already lined up."

I turn bright red and make sure not to look across the locker room in Keith's direction. "No, I don't. I just kind of like the idea of spending some time by myself in my own house with no one around to bother me or break the silence."

Danny shudders. "Silence—brr! No, thank you."

I shut my locker. "See you gorillas later. Try not to slam any poetry too hard, Ellis. You wouldn't want to have to call a paramedic for that."

"I definitely wouldn't. In fact, I think I'll go cold turkey on the poetry for the rest of my life. It will be safer that way."

Brooke and Naomi howl with protest and I take that opening to skedaddle. I get out to my car, put my duffel bag in the back seat, and get behind the wheel when I get a text from Brooke with the details on the poetry slam.

It sounds fun, but I don't really feel like being around a crowd—not after I just went out to the club last night. That leads me to thinking about Keith again and I push the thought out of my head to concentrate on driving home.

The rest of the crew pulls out first, and by the time I get around to switching on the engine, nothing happens. I turn the key again and again. The dashboard lights come on, but the engine just clicks.

"Damn it!" I whisper under my breath and pop the hood.

I peer into the engine compartment like that could actually tell me something I don't already know. I have a dead battery and, to make matters worse, not only do I not have a set of jumper cables to jumpstart it, no one is around to let me use their car to jumpstart it.

I glance around the parking lot, and just when I think this situation couldn't get any more disastrous, right then, the firehouse alarm goes off.

The garage rolls open and the rescue truck, ambulance, and John's support pickup pull out onto the street before driving away. Great. The whole crew is gone along with all their vehicles. I'm alone with a dead car battery.

Chapter 10: Leila

I say a few more bad words and pull out my phone. I get ready to call Triple-A to jumpstart my car when Keith walks around the corner and sees me. "Hey!" he calls. "What's the problem?"

"My battery is dead. I was just about to call Triple-A."

"Don't bother," he tells me. "I'll get it started for you."

"You don't have to do that."

"I know I don't. Put your phone away."

He throws his duffel bag into his truck bed, opens the driver's door, and starts rooting around behind the driver's seat.

"Aren't you going to pull your truck over?" I ask. "You're too far away for jumper cables to reach."

"I don't have jumper cables," he tells me over his shoulder. "I have something better."

He straightens up, takes a big charger out of the back seat of his truck, and brings it over to my car. I gape at the box in his hand. "You drive around....with *that?*"

"Sure. You never know when your battery might die somewhere with no one around. Besides, it really sucks going door to door looking for someone to give you a jump....like now." He sets the charger on top of my radiator and clamps the cables to my battery. "Try it now."

I sit down behind the wheel, turn the ignition, and the car roars to life. "You might want to leave it running for a while," he tells me while he unclamps the cables. "Give the battery a chance to recharge."

"Thanks," I exclaim. "You Brewers really know your stuff, don't you?"

He shoots me a grin. "If you want something done, get a couple of Brewers involved."

"I'll remember that." I find myself blushing again. "You're a life-saver."

I realize as soon as I say it that he really is one, and without meaning to, I glance down at his mouth.

I look up to find him scrutinizing me with unusual intensity and then, before I can even blink, we're kissing again the way we did outside the club.

His fingers slide into my hair and my body dissolves in this cloud of passion and aching desire, but it goes so far beyond that.

He means so much to me and I channel all that feeling into kissing him. We both might decide tomorrow that it will be better for everyone if we just stay friends.

If we do, I need to appreciate this moment for as long as it lasts. I need for him to understand that I'm not just fooling around by kissing him. I really mean it—whatever it is that I really mean.

I already knew what Chris said about any woman being lucky to get with him, so why shouldn't that be me?

As soon as I think that, the emotion and desire erupts out of me as never before. I want to be that woman. I want him.

I throw myself into kissing him with everything I have and he responds just as hard. He swivels me around and pins me against the car the way he did last night. His body hardens all the way down to his hips. He wants it just as much as I do.

I don't have to wonder if he's serious about starting something with me. He wouldn't start it at all if he wasn't serious. He's been making comments and dropping hints for days.

Now it's happening and we both know it's happening. His hands slide down to my waist and then behind me. He scoops me up and crushes me into his pelvis even as he drills me against my car.

The engine vibrations buzz through the metal behind me. The car is still running and we're still in the firehouse parking lot.

We both seem to wake up to the fact at the same moment. As soon as the crew gets back from their call, they'll see us here.

Keith slides his fingers into my hair again and clenches his fist, but he doesn't either pull me away from his mouth or push me into it. He keeps kissing me for a minute and then whispers, "Come home with me."

I drown in those words as his lips send me back into a hypnotic dream. If I go to his place, it's all over for both of us. I won't leave it—not in any meaningful way.

My heart leaps at the thought of actually getting together with him. I should have been with him all along.

Part of me thinks we really have been together all along. We've been as close as we possibly could be. We know everything about each other and we both care about each other as the most important people in our lives. Only the sex was missing.

What's about to happen goes way beyond that. We haven't been together all along because I wasn't his and he wasn't mine. We're about to embark on a whole new world of feeling and commitment.

I want that more than anything, but I don't seem to be able to break the spell of his lips. I never want to stop kissing him, not even to go home with him. I never want this moment to end.

A car drives past on the street in front of the firehouse. That sound of engine noise brings us both back to our senses. The fire crew isn't coming back yet, but they will soon.

Keith pulls away, whispers, "Meet me at my place," turns to my car, takes his charger off the radiator, sets it on the ground, and slams the hood shut before he takes the charger back to his pickup.

I can't look at him or the reality will really start to set in. I get behind the wheel, back my car out of the parking lot, and start driving. I'm not going home. I'm going to Keith's apartment.

I've never been there before. I've never even driven down his street before, but I know where he lives.

He lives in a nice building on the other side of town. When I pull into the parking lot, I see him getting out of his truck on the west end of the lot. He must have taken a different route to get here.

I switch off my car without thinking about it first. I should have left it running. Oh, well. I can just ask him to give me another jumpstart.

I walk over to where he stands waiting for me on the sidewalk. The minute I get near him, he slips his hand into mine, threads our fingers together, and kisses me right there on the street corner for anyone to see.

No one we know is watching, but the implications couldn't be clearer. He really means for this to be serious. I want that, too, but my stomach turns a somersault at the thought. We're doing this. We're really going there.

He leads me by the hand and we walk into the building lobby. He presses the elevator button and his eyes flash when he looks down into mine. I can't believe I'm actually about to do this.

The elevator dings, we step inside, and as soon as the doors close, Keith uses my arm to pull me in and starts kissing me again. We kiss as passionately as before, but it seems so much more important this time.

I slide my hand around the back of his neck. He feels strong, but much softer than I remember. His strength doesn't make him dangerous like Damon's does.

Keith stands back and stares down at me while the elevator glides the rest of the way to his floor. I don't even see which floor it is. I can't tear my gaze away from his eyes.

He seems to slow down as we get closer to the moment of truth. That's the way he is. He always controls himself. He would rather go slowly than make a mistake from rushing.

I tremble and he feels it through my arm. He squeezes my hand and I squeeze back, but there's no backing out now.

The elevator dings again and the doors slide open. He steps out and escorts me down a long, carpeted hall to his apartment door, where he unlocks it with his key.

He holds the door open for me to enter and I walk into an immaculate two-bedroom apartment. Big windows in the living room overlooking even nicer neighborhoods. The street beyond the parking lot leads toward downtown Howe in the distance.

A telescope stands on a tripod by the windows and he has a pullup bar set up across the doorway leading to his bedroom.

A huge, chocolate-brown leather sofa set takes up most of the rest of the living room with a glass coffee table between the sofa, armchair, and loveseat. A desktop computer sits on the desk in the corner.

He even has a glass bowl with polished sea rocks in the bottom and a bunch of dried, spiky desert vegetation sticking out of the top. It makes a very attractive centerpiece in the middle of the coffee table.

I spot a few pieces of blown-glass sculpture dotted around the apartment. I don't know why I should find it surprising that his apartment looks so well kept and elegant. I should have known he would be too exacting to live in a grungy old bachelor pad.

I get fascinated by the telescope and wander over to it. What does he see when he looks through it? Does he look at the stars? I can't envision him spying on people in other houses.

He comes up behind me, puts his arms around me, and buries his face in my neck. I get another electric thrill that I'm here with him, but then I burst out laughing.

"What's so funny?" he rumbles.

"Your beard—it tickles."

"Don't tell me you're going to start having a problem with my beard, because if I have to choose, you're outta here."

I laugh and turn around to face him. "No.....I like it."

I touch his face and he smiles. His eyes look so much softer and express so much more depth than I ever noticed before. Maybe he never let himself express it before.

I can't help but kiss him when he looks at me like that, and before I know it, he wraps his arms around my waist and lifts my feet off the floor.

I let myself go in the power of his embrace. I don't have to hold myself back anymore. We're alone together and no one will interrupt.

I wrap my legs around his waist to hold myself up while we kiss and he backs toward the loveseat. He sits down on it with me straddling him and my body bursts into flame when we kiss.

We're both still wearing our uniforms, and when I touch his chest, I feel how powerful he is under his T-shirt.

He leans forward to pull off his jacket. Then, when he leans back and I fall into his kiss, he starts tugging off *my* jacket.

My nerves stand on end when I realize he's undressing me—for *that.* We didn't come here just to kiss.

I open my eyes to find his intense stare burning into me from inches away. He watches my every reaction as he pulls my jacket off and starts unbuttoning my shirt.

Every graze of his fingertips through my shirt excites me out of my mind. We're actually going to do it. His eyes tell me so in no uncertain terms. I wouldn't be inside his apartment right now for any other reason.

His eyes dip to my collar and he watches his own hands working down my shirt as he unfastens one button after another. The cooler air hits my skin. He can see me in my bra now.

His eyes drift back up to me and the world stands still as he slides my shirt off my shoulders. I tremble before those eyes as he peels the shirt down my arms and lays it aside.

I can't stand the way he's looking at me, so I hide by kissing him again. He doesn't try to stop me. He lets me lay my bare skin on his chest until, out of nowhere, he flicks my bra clasp undone.

It falls open and my body responds as never before. Every part of me lies exposed to him now. My skin, my body—my whole being—they all belong to him now.

He slips my bra off and then tears his lips away from my mouth. Before I even realize what he's doing, he dives into my chest and his mouth closes on my left breast.

I gasp as unstoppable sensation shoots through me. I can't move except to drive my body down on him even harder. All thought of getting away or doing something else evaporates out of my mind. I succumb to him. I can never escape because I don't want to.

He holds me in his mouth as I gasp and moan in the throes of ecstatic agony. He pushes off the couch just long enough to yank his T-shirt over his head and my skin goes on fire all over again when my skin touches his skin.

The hair on his chest tingles all my nerve endings, but his mouth sends me over the edge into madness. I can't handle the mind-blowing sensations of him touching me, circling his big hands on my hips, and rotating me on his hardening crotch.

I moan again and both my hands fly to his head. I pull him in and struggle against all the warring sensations he's giving me. I can't stop the desire skyrocketing me out of this world.

He exhales and his hot breath on my skin makes me so much hungrier for him. Every touch, every breath, every movement makes me more fully his.

He rips off my breast with an agonized gasp of his own, grabs my waistband, and starts unbuttoning my pants. I need him too badly to just sit here and wait for him to do it.

I clasp both hands around his face and lift his head to kiss him. His hair has become disheveled while we've been kissing. It hangs in his eyes and makes him look a hundred times more intoxicatingly attractive.

My fingers sink into his beard and I kiss him with every ounce of desire coursing through me.

He doesn't stop unbuttoning my pants and then unzipping them. I explode and grab his belt. I can't get his clothes off fast enough. I want to see and feel everything that he is.

He reacts to that and pulls away from me. He leans back, spreads his arms, and doesn't interfere while I unbuckle his belt, unbutton his pants, and slide the zipper down. I can already feel him throbbing underneath.

He looks so much more powerful like this with his shirt off. His eyes harden, but I can't pull his pants down when I'm sitting on his lap.

He immediately takes over and lifts himself and me off the couch just for an instant—just long enough to slide his pants down past his knees.

Now I can feel his whole body, but he doesn't give me a chance to enjoy it. He grabs my pants and yanks them down. He hesitates only long enough for me to rise up on my knees so he can push my pants down, too.

I want to kiss him and touch him. I want to do everything with him, but he takes over again, circles his chiseled arm around my waist, and rotates both of us off the couch.

He somehow manages to shove the coffee table far enough out of the way to land on his knees, sits me down on the couch, and pushes between my knees before his lips cover my mouth.

I get lost in kissing him for a minute before I realize that I'm sitting naked on the couch with him kneeling between my spread thighs.

He doesn't give me a chance to catch my breath before I feel his hard rod touching me….and then he pushes his way in.

I gasp and then scream as his thickness splits me apart. The intense sensation blasts me into the stratosphere, but there's no stopping him. He grabs me behind my back, pulls me to the very edge of the couch, and then slides me down on top of him as he sits back on his heels.

I scream again and again as he pumps up into me from below. He's so mind-blowingly hard and he drives in with such unstoppable determination that I can't stand it.

He tries to kiss me, but I can't bring myself to respond. I can't cope and I scream with every thrust, but he still doesn't stop.

I open my eyes just long enough to see him glaring at me from below. His body moves in a mesmerizing rhythm of muscle and power. My being dissolves in his grasp as he pumps all these earth-shattering sensations through me.

I can't even think until, a second later, he grasps my chin in one strong hand and turns my head to face him. He draws my mouth to his lips and now I can't tear my eyes away from his.

He stares so penetratingly into my soul that I collapse in another agony of disintegrating intensity. I can't look away. I'm his now. That's what this means. His eyes wipe out all doubt. It's all over between us.

He keeps rising on his knees just enough to shatter my body on his iron spike. Every thrust blows me to kingdom come. I don't know what's happening to me, but whatever it is, I can't stop it. I don't want to stop it. I want to be his. I want everything he'll do to me.

I barely notice when he scoops his arms under my seat, clamps my body down on him, and gets to his feet with me still clinging to him for dear life.

I can't stop sobbing and moaning in desperation, but he never lets me go. He keeps kissing me and holding me against him when he stands up, kicks off his shoes and pants, and carries me into his bedroom.

He sits down on the edge of the bed with me on his lap. I whimper and whine every time another spasm drives me down on top of him. I can't help myself as one wave after another wipes out everything but him.

He kisses me when I need to kiss him. He touches me all over, plays with my body, and guides my rhythm when I can't stop another blast of climactic energy sweeping away everything I know.

I finally collapse on his chest and he kisses my hair. I can't think anymore. I don't need to think as long as I'm here with him. Everything will be okay just like he said. It has to be because he's here.

He encloses me in his arms and leans back on the bed. I fall on top of him still reeling in the clouds. Sitting in this position turns me on so much that I could escalate to another orgasmic overload if something doesn't change.

My lips fall on his chest and I crawl my ravenous mouth up his neck to his ears. I want to devour him. I want to exhaust his strength by pulverizing him with my desire, but just then, he clamps his arms around me and rolls me onto my back.

He never slips out of me and then, in a split second, he's on top drilling me to infinity again. Will this ever end?

Chapter 11: Keith

I wake up, and before I even open my eyes, I smell Leila. She lies on top of me with her sweet thighs spread on either side of my hips. Her head lies on my shoulder and the rest of her magnificent naked body covers me.

That smell reminds me of everything we did yesterday and last night. I stayed conscious just long enough to pull the bedspread over us before we both passed out.

Now she's still here and sound asleep on top of me. I do a quick mental calculation. Today is Saturday. I have to work the evening shift starting at three o'clock this afternoon. She has the day off.

Things are different between us now. That's what last night meant. I don't have to ask her to know it's true. This is real. It's as real as I ever could have hoped for it to be. We both matter to each other too much. We wouldn't have gone this far if it wasn't real.

I don't know what time it is and I don't want to wake her up by turning my head to look at the clock. Either way, I have enough time to lie here and enjoy this before I have to go back on duty.

I'm just relaxing in for a long wait when she stiffens, groans, and then squirms, but she doesn't sit up. She buries her face deeper under my hair and nuzzles into my neck. Her whole body shudders against me

.

I twist my head around and kiss her on the temple. That's the only part of her I can reach.

She clears her throat in my ear and then mumbles under her breath, "You have to work today, don't you?"

"Not until later. You can relax."

She only hesitates for a second, groans again, and rolls off me, but she leaves one leg lying across my waist and cuddles her silky body into my side. She presses her face back into my neck and wraps her arms around me. "What time is it?"

"I don't know." I crane my head up, now that she's awake. "It's eleven-thirty."

She groans a third time and I laugh. "I'm getting too old for this," she growls.

"Get used to it, sweetie." I turn on my side and kiss her on the mouth this time. Everything about her smells and tastes heavenly.

She grumbles, "I should have known you would be a slave driver," but she tightens her arms around my neck and drapes her whole body against me while we kiss.

"We should get up and make some breakfast before you go home," I tell her. "We'll both need to refuel after last night."

Her eyes drift open. Did they ever look this bright? "Breakfast? Don't you mean dinner?"

I laugh again. She makes me so happy. "I'm going to take a shower. You can stay there if you want to."

I go take a shower, and when I get back, she's still lounging in bed watching me change into a clean uniform.

She looks delicious lying in my bed all naked, but it's going to be like this from now on—one of us going to work and leaving the other one alone—when we aren't working together. John might even decide to schedule us on opposing shifts. I wouldn't be surprised.

I can't remember him ever doing that with any other couple, but I can't remember any other couple working on the fire crew before. I don't know what his policies are on that. Maybe I should find out before he finds out about us.

I buckle my belt and sit down on the edge of the bed to kiss Leila. "Do you want to stay here for the rest of the day?"

"I should go home," she replies. "I have some stuff to do there."

"Do you want to leave now or do you want to wait a while?"

"I'll leave with you. I don't feel right about staying in your apartment when you aren't here."

I laugh at that, too. "What—do you plan to steal my TV or something?'

"No, silly." She playfully swats my shoulder. "I already have a TV. I don't need another one. I was planning on stealing your computer."

I can't stop laughing. "You can have it."

"Stop it. I wouldn't steal your stuff." She climbs out of bed and I have to stand aside and take in the sights when she struts across my bedroom to the bathroom. The shower switches on and I go out to the kitchen to make breakfast.

She's right. It's too late for breakfast, so I end up making us some grilled cheese sandwiches instead.

She comes out with her hair all wet. She doesn't have any other clothes, so she's dressed in her uniform again.

"So...." I begin when I put her plate in front of her. "Can I see you again?"

She shoots me a blushing smirk. "Twist my arm."

"How about tonight? Do you have any plans—any hot dates you might want to go on?"

She laughs. "Yeah, I have a hot date with a buff, studly firefighter from Howe Station. You better be careful or he'll beat you up if he finds out about us."

"I can't wait to meet him."

We both share the joke while we finish our food. "So….." I go on. "I could pick you up after work."

"You get off at midnight," she points out.

"Yeah? You just said you didn't have any plans—unless your firefighter boyfriend is going to be there."

She bursts into giggles. "How about we just stay at my place tonight? I'll leave the door open for you."

"Because you'll already be asleep?" I ask. "Is that what you mean?"

"I will definitely be asleep. I'll need to catch up after last night."

I feel the blood rush to my cheeks. "Maybe I should do the same thing. If I went to your place, neither of us would get any sleep."

"My point exactly."

I bend across the table to kiss her before I pick up both of our plates. "Maybe us getting together tonight isn't such a great idea."

"Only if you can give me an iron-clad guarantee that we're going to sleep instead of fooling around."

"I wouldn't want to promise something I know I can't deliver. I have to go. Walk down with me."

I take the dishes to the kitchen and she calls after me, "Why do you have to leave so soon? It isn't even one o'clock yet."

"There's something I have to do," I call back.

"What is it?"

I come out of the kitchen and level her with a direct look. "I have to go see John….about all of this."

Her smile evaporates. "Do you have to?"

"Yes, I have to. He's my brother and our boss. He needs to know everything that might affect how the firehouse operates. I would have to tell him even without that. He asked me point blank the other day if anything was going on between us and I said there wasn't. I can't have him thinking I lied to him."

She looks away with such a stricken expression that I can't keep away from her. I cross the living room to slip my hand into hers.

"Don't worry," I murmur. "You know John. He'll be good about it and so will the rest of the fire crew. If this is real, they're all going to find out about it pretty soon anyway. They might as well find out now."

She looks up at me with eyes swimming with emotion. I have to kiss her.

I squeeze her hand one more time. "Come on. I'll walk you down to your car and see if you need another jump."

We head for the door, but just as I'm locking it behind us, she murmurs under her breath, "I will definitely need another jump."

I laugh at the joke and we both go back to our old light-hearted banter until I kiss her goodbye at the curb and she drives away. Now comes the hard part.

I drive to John's house and sit in my truck for a while to work up my courage to go inside.

His car sits in the driveway. I don't see Ellen's car, which means she's gone out somewhere. I pray to God that Oakleigh isn't home, either. I need to see John alone.

I glance at my watch. It's one-thirty. I need to do this now or I might be late for work.

I force myself to go up to the door. I feel like I should knock and wait for him to answer, but I've never done that before.

I walk in and see the patio doors open to the backyard. I hear him banging around out there, and when I go outside, I find him tinkering with the barbecue with his open toolbox next to him.

He looks up. "Howdy. What's the good word?"

I sit down at the picnic table near him. How should I put this?

He looks up and narrows his eyes. "Is there a good word?"

I shrug. "Remember when you asked me if anything was going on between me and Leila?"

"Yeah?"

"Well, there is—now. It wasn't before, but it is now. I just didn't want you to think I lied to you about it."

He bends over the barbecue and goes back to what he's doing. "That was fast."

"Yeah, well.....I guess it was a long time coming."

"You can say that again." He looks up, scowls, and then bursts into a smirk. "It couldn't happen to a nicer guy. You two deserve each other."

I look away. "Thanks."

"So what do you want me to do about it?"

"You tell me. Do you have to do anything about it? I wasn't sure if you needed to separate us onto different shifts....or what."

"Do I need to separate you onto different shifts?"

"No! I mean, I don't know your policy on couples working together...."

"I don't have a policy on couples except for the one that says couples who are of different ranks aren't allowed to work for the department. That was the problem between me and Ellen, remember?"

"Yeah, but that doesn't apply to me and Leila. We're of equal rank."

"You're senior to her, but other than that, I don't see a problem....unless you think there will be."

"I don't think there will be."

"Then there's no problem."

I don't know what to say. I didn't expect him to make this so easy for me—for us.

He reads my mind. "Look, I don't know what you were expecting, but you two have always been close. You've been closer than anyone else who has ever worked for me. I'm only surprised you two didn't get together before now."

My head shoots up. "Really?"

"Yes. I was honestly surprised when she got together with Damon—only slightly less surprised than how okay you were with it."

"Why wouldn't I be okay with it? I thought he was all right—then."

"That's what I mean. It never crossed your mind that something might happen between you, but I can't be the only one who saw you two getting together. I know Ellen did."

My jaw drops in astonishment. "Did she tell you that?"

"Yes. She told me that night after we left the pool hall."

"She never said anything while we were there. From the way she was talking ....."

"She had to say that. I'm the fire chief and she's my wife. She's also your sister-in-law. She couldn't come right out and tell you and Leila that you should be together. Fortunately, the other paramedics said it instead, but Ellen was definitely thinking it."

I can't answer that, either. This completely changes everything.

Why didn't I see this? Leila didn't see it, either. Why not?

He stands up, puts his tools back in the box, and comes over to me. He lays his hand on my shoulder. "I can't say this as your chief, so let me say it as your brother. Congratulations. I'm happy—for both of you. You both deserve it, especially after the crap she just went through with Damon. You've been on your own for too long and she's perfect for you. I don't see a problem with you two continuing to work together, but if it becomes a problem, I'm sure one of us will say so and we can shuffle things around."

I can't look at him, so I look down at my hands. "Thanks."

He squeezes my shoulder tighter. "You should probably get going or you'll be late for your shift."

I stand up planning to just walk away. I don't trust myself to say anything. My throat hurts. I've never been so grateful to have him as a brother and a boss.

Just before I turn away, I catch one fleeting glimpse of his eyes. That one look breaks the dam and we both throw our arms around each other. I clasp him in a tight hug that doesn't last nearly long enough.

I finally force myself to step away, but I can't speak above a whisper when I say, "Thanks," again.

"You bet." He claps me on the shoulder. "Have a good shift. Call me if you or the crew need anything."

Chapter 12: Leila

I drive home to my house, walk inside, dump my stuff on the couch, and switch on my computer. I putter around putting stuff away and taking off my uniform while the computer boots up.

I check the time. It's almost three o'clock and I usually Skype with my parents in Oklahoma on my days off. I open the app, but they aren't online yet. I'll just have to wait.

My body sags with exhaustion from staying up nearly all night long with Keith. I will definitely need to sleep tonight.

I can't help but get butterflies when I think about him. He's probably done telling John about us. Now Keith is on his way back to the firehouse for his shift.

I don't worry about John or the crew finding out about me and Keith, especially not after the comments everyone was making at the pool hall and afterward.

I go into the kitchen and take out a few things to make for dinner. I haven't spent an evening like this on my own since I got together with Damon.

Tonight should be peaceful and calm, now that I don't have to worry about him anymore. I'm going to enjoy talking to my parents, maybe reading a book, and then crawling into bed early.

I check the app again, but my parents are still not online, so I send them a text asking if they're ready to call. I don't get an answer right away. Maybe they're out doing something. Maybe they're working in the garden.

I go into my bedroom, change out of my uniform into my old tattered grey sweatpants and an oversized T-shirt, and put on my slippers even though it's only three o'clock in the afternoon.

I pick out what book I'm going to read and take it back to the living room. My parents are still not online.

I put the book on the couch and head back to the kitchen when the front door bursts open. My surprise turns to fury when Damon storms in without knocking.

"What are you doing here?" I demand. "You have no right to be here. We're finished! When are you going to get that through your head?"

"You can't just dump me, Leila," he counters. "We have to talk about this."

"There's nothing to talk about. You knocked me around one too many times. You disrespected my boss and my colleagues. You behaved like a jerk in front of the whole fire crew. Now it's over between us. Talking about it won't change that."

"Don't play hardball with me. Whatever happened between us, we can work it out."

"No, we can't. Now leave before I call the Police."

He laughs in my face. "I am the Police, darling. I'm already here."

I glare at him. He's really going to make this as difficult as it can possibly be, but I realize right then that I left my phone in the pocket of my uniform jacket. It's on the couch with my handbag, duffel bag, and keys.

Damon blocks me from getting to it, so I decide to put the kitchen counter between us. I go back into the kitchen and pretend to start making dinner.

He strides over to the counter, but he doesn't enter the kitchen with me. He keeps his distance, too. "Where the hell have you been? I've been looking everywhere for you. I must have come by at least four times last night and you weren't here. I was worried sick about you."

"You don't need to worry about me anymore, Damon. What I do isn't your concern."

"Just tell me where you were. I drove all over town searching for you."

I shouldn't tell him the truth, but I want to hurt him. I want to shove it in his face that it's over between us. I want to make him realize once and for all that we are never getting back together—ever.

"I spent the night with Keith Brewer……"

I realize a second later that something isn't right with my head. My vision isn't working right and I don't seem to be facing the same way I was before.

I don't believe the truth until I see Damon's fist fly past my head going a million miles an hour. I can't imagine how he got to me that fast, but the minute my head finishes snapping sideways, he punches me again going the other way.

I reel and fall across the kitchen floor. My ears ring. I can't make out the words Damon is yelling at me from above.

I taste blood in my mouth, but my brain feels so fuzzy that nothing makes sense. My phone. I have to get to my phone. I have to call for help.

I crawl out of the kitchen and hear Damon bellowing at me. He curses me, calls me a tramp and a bunch of other nasty names, and then I see his boot flying toward me from the side.

It flashes in my peripheral vision before it connects with the side of my head, but I'm already so out of it that I hardly feel it. It doesn't hurt the way it should.

He kicks my body multiple times on the way to the living room. The phone. I have to get to the phone.

I definitely feel the blows to my body, but the pain only triggers an adrenaline response that makes me crawl faster. My vision clears just enough for me to spot my jacket lying on the couch.

Damon strides around me and delivers another vicious kick to my head. The impact hurls me onto my back, but at least now I'm lying right next to the couch.

He stands over me kicking me again and again. I don't allow myself to look at him. I'll lose my nerve if I do.

I summon the last of my strength, lunge for my jacket, and grab my phone just as he delivers another brutal strike to the side of my head. My skull cracks against the corner of the couch and I punch the emergency call button right before I pass out.

Chapter 13: Keith

I march into the firehouse garage to find George Dow, Vince Jaeger, Drew Killian, and Cameron Santiago already there.

They all turn around to greet me. "Hey, man!" Drew calls out. "Long time, no see!"

"Yeah, it's been a while since I worked the third shift." I pull up and survey them all. Sophie, Jessie, and Brooke are our scheduled paramedics with Drew scheduled as Brooke's backup EMT on the ambulance.

"Is it true Danny saw a ghost on a call last week?" Vince asks me.

I snort at him. "Are you actually asking me if something Danny said was 'true'?" I put air quotes around that word. "I thought you people knew better than that."

They all laugh. "Hey, maybe we'll see a ghost on this shift," George suggests.

"Just do what Danny does and make one up," Jessie tells him and they laugh some more.

"Are you gonna drive the truck this shift?" Cameron asks me. "You always drive on the second shift, don't you?"

I raise both hands. "I'm not here to step on anyone's toes. You drive if that's the way you want to play it."

"I don't want to get in any kind of trouble with the boss."

"As if he would get you in trouble for doing your job," I reply. "Drive. I don't care as long as we make it to the call in one piece."

Talk turns to other matters and we get busy checking the trucks, resupplying what needs to be resupplied, and then Vince pulls the rescue truck out into the driveway to wash it.

"Don't forget to scrub behind your ears while you're at it!" Jessie yells.

"How about you come help me and I'll spray you down with the hose?" he calls back and the crew laughs some more.

Cameron gets a phone call just then and goes into the locker room to take it. I'm going through the rescue truck when Andy Skinner comes over to me and holds out a package. "This just came in. I think it's the bag for the new jump kit."

"Hey, Sophie!" I holler. "Do you want to fit out the new jump kit?"

"Shouldn't we leave that for Chris and Leila?" she asks. "I don't want to set it up wrong."

"You're the one who's going to be using it. If they want to change it, they can do that when they come back on duty. You might as well have a new jump kit while you're at it."

She shuffles her feet and pushes the bag back at me. "I'll wait. I can use the spare kit until they fit it out."

"It's up to you." I stick the new bag in the back seat where Chris and Leila usually sit. They'll find it there the next time they work on the truck.

I turn back to my checklist and Vince and George show up stretching out the hose to wash down the truck. I make myself scarce so I don't get hit by flying spray, but right then, the firehouse alarm goes off.

It echoes through the neighborhood and the whole crew comes rushing back. "So much for your annual shower, Vince!" Brooke yells. "You'll have to wait for next year."

He's just opening his mouth to give her his smartass comeback when Cameron hops into the cab next to me. "Let's rock and roll!"

The paramedics load up and he pulls the truck out. Drew follows behind in the ambulance, but John's support truck isn't with us—not today. He'll roll out if we need him, but we should be able to handle things on our own unless the world really comes to an end.

"What's the address?!" Cameron yells over the siren.

I check the notes from dispatch. "The call is a medical—domestic assault! Police are on scene and the premises are secure. The perp is gone, but the victim is still there."

"The address!" Cameron repeats. "Spare me the gory details. Just tell me where I'm going."

I turn to the next page on the screen and my throat goes dry when I see the address. It's Leila's house. Damn it. I should have seen this coming. I should have made her stay at my place......forever?

I wouldn't be able to keep her locked up, not even for her own protection. Damon would have found a way to get to her no matter what I did.....which means he'll keep doing it as long as both he and Leila are still alive.

The bastard. It's lucky for him he isn't at her place anymore. I wouldn't trust myself not to end him then and there.

"Keith!!" Cameron hollers. "What's the address?! Where are we going?"

I give him the address as best I can, but I hear my voice shaking. I hate to think what I'll find when I get to Leila's house. I never should have let her out of my sight—not with that fiend running loose.

"Is something wrong?" George calls from the back seat. "Is something wrong with the call?'

I turn around very slowly. I don't want to say the words, but this crew needs to know before they walk in to find one of their own on the floor. "It's Leila. The victim is Leila."

Dead silence answers me from the back. The two paramedics gape at me in horror and then Vince grits his teeth, turns to glare out the window, and mutters under his breath, "I knew it! I knew that asshole would try something like this."

I don't want to know how Vince knew about Damon and Leila. I turn back to the front, and thank the stars, Cameron gets on the radio and alerts Brooke and Drew that we're attending a domestic assault with Leila as the victim.

We pull up in front of Leila's house. Everything looks normal except for a few dozen cops swarming all over the place.

They direct Drew into the driveway, but Cameron parks the firetruck at the curb. I doubt we'll need the truck. The ambulance is going to be more important.

Sophie and Jessie get out and the rest of us guys enter the house with them. A bunch of cops stand around Leila, who is lying on the living room floor in a pool of blood. She's out cold and no wonder.

Her head is a mass of bruises with blood coming out of her nose, ears, and mouth. Her face is completely unrecognizable.

I stand off to one side as the three paramedics surround her all talking and working on her all at once. I hear the other firefighters talking to the cops....and then I notice some of them gathered around Leila's computer in the corner.

I just happen to glance over there and spot them playing back a video feed on Leila's Skype app. "It was turned on during the attack," one of the officers murmurs in a hushed undertone. "It captured the whole thing on video."

I catch one glimpse of Damon kicking Leila and I force myself to look away. I can't watch that, but at least it's obvious to everyone who did this.

"Bring in the gurney....and full spinal immobilization gear," Brooke orders over her shoulder.

Vince and George hustle outside to get the stuff from the truck. It's a good thing they do because I can't move. I can only stand here rooted to the spot and stare down at Leila.

This is my fault. I should have protected her. I should have been there. I should have known something like this was going to happen.

Even Vince knew something like this was going to happen. I was too out of my mind with happiness over finally getting together with Leila. I didn't think clearly enough to realize that Damon wouldn't accept the inevitable.

The other guys help the paramedics immobilize Leila, load her onto a gurney, and take her out to the waiting ambulance. Jessie and Sophie pile into the ambulance with Brooke while Drew gets behind the wheel.

Just before he pulls out, something snaps inside me and I hop into the front passenger seat. "Go back to the firehouse!" I tell Cameron. "I'm going to the hospital. Don't worry. I'll call John and explain everything. Just get everyone back on shift and cover the firehouse while I'm gone."

He nods and Drew peels out of the driveway with his lights flashing and sirens wailing. Going to the hospital with Leila is against firehouse policy. I should stay on shift, too, but no force on Earth is going to keep me away from her—not now.

I can't hear myself think over the siren, so I send John a text. *I need you to come down to Howe General Hospital immediately. It's an emergency.* If that doesn't bring him running, nothing will.

There's nothing for me to do when I get there except to stand off to one side and watch the three paramedics hand Leila over to the hospital staff.

They only do the briefest check on her before they rush her off to surgery. Then the ambulance crew has to resupply from the hospital, fill out their paperwork, and go back to the firehouse, too.

"I'm staying here," I tell Naomi. "John is on his way. I'll explain everything to him, but I'm not going back on shift. I'm staying here."

She stares up at me with huge eyes. I can just imagine what she sees when she looks at my face. "Uh...okay. You work it out with John." Her eyes dart behind me. "Keep us updated on her progress, okay?"

I nod at nothing. "Yeah. Sure."

She scampers and takes the other three with her. That leaves me free to go upstairs to the surgical theater waiting room. I'm the only person in here.

I sit down in the chairs and look down at my hands. This is my fault. I should have done something. I should have taken the day off to spend with her. I never should have left her alone.

I completely lose track of time. It might be hours later when John walks in. "I just got the call from Jim at the Police Department. They have a warrant out for Damon's arrest, but they don't know where he is." He stops dead in his tracks when he sees me sitting there with my shoulders bowed.

He studies me and then sits down next to me. I can't look at him. "I'm gonna need to take some time off work...." I croak.

"Of course. Take all the time you need."

I wave my hand at nothing. "You'll....have to explain it....to the rest of the crew....."

"I'm sure they'll understand."

I don't reply. I've never felt this rotten in my life. How could I go from being so blissfully happy last night....to this?

"Whatever you do, don't start blaming yourself for this," John tells me. "This isn't your fault. You had to go to work. You couldn't stay with her around the clock and you won't be able to do it now."

"Oh, I can do it now," I counter. "I can definitely do it now."

"You won't be able to do it when she goes back to work. You have to let her live her life and you have to live yours. You can't keep her locked in a cage twenty-four-seven."

I don't answer that, either. I hate hearing my own thoughts coming out of his mouth, but one thing he says rings in my ears.

She will get out of the hospital. She will recover from this....and then we'll be together.

We'll get through this and then I swear to God I will never let anything like this happen again.

John says a few other reassuring things, but I don't listen. I can only concentrate on that one thing. Leila will get out of the hospital. We will have a life after this—just as soon as the Police put Damon away.

Chapter 14: Leila

I wake up feeling like absolute hell. I can't even open my eyes and I don't want to. Everything hurts and I don't have any problem remembering why.

I try to sit up and look around. Is Damon still here? Is he going to come after me again?

Someone touches my hand. "Take it easy, sweetheart," a gruff male voice murmurs not far away. "Don't make any sudden moves. Your head is still swollen up like a balloon."

"Keith?" I look everywhere, but I can't see a thing. "I can't see! What's wrong with me?"

"You're okay," he murmurs and pets my hand between both of his. I remember those hands so well. "Your eyelids are too swollen, but the swelling will go down and you'll be all right. The doctors did surgery on your brain and they say you're going to make a full recovery."

I collapse back on my pillows. I really wish I could see him, but I feel him sit down next to me on the mattress. I even feel his beard when he kisses my hand. "Damon....he showed up at my house....."

"I know all about it, sweetie," he breathes. "You were on Skype when it happened. The app took a video of the whole attack. The Police have the video in evidence and there's a warrant out for Damon's arrest."

I heave a sigh. Even breathing hurts. "How did you.....?" I think fast. "You....you were on duty....when it happened....."

"We all were. We all attended the call. The crew has been in here a few different times to see you. Everyone is waiting to hear how you're doing. You have the whole crew pulling for you."

"And.....shouldn't you be at work right now?"

"No, I shouldn't be. John put me on indefinite leave until you get better."

I cringe. I don't want Keith missing work because of me....and then I realize that I do want that. I want exactly that. I want to be so important to him that he'll miss work to sit by my hospital bed.

I shut my eyes and open them again. That's when my eyelids part enough for me to see him sitting there.

He isn't wearing his uniform. Of course not. He wears the same casual jeans, T-shirt, and leather jacket he had on at the club. His hair is wet and combed back from his face.

I want to burst into a huge, beaming smile when I see him, but my face doesn't function right. "Hey."

He grins broadly enough for both of us. "Hey. Welcome back."

"I'm sorry....you had to see that....."

"Don't be. I'm just sorry you had to go through it. I should have kept you at my place...."

"No," I insist. "I wouldn't want to hide from him. I have to live my life. Anyway, if he gets arrested, we won't have to worry about him."

Keith looks away. He doesn't say what we're both thinking.

If Damon gets arrested, he won't stay in jail. Assault isn't a serious enough offense to get him put away for any significant length of time.

Damon hasn't even been arrested yet. He's still out there running around free. My eyes dart toward the door. How long will it take him to come after me again?

"I.....I screwed up, Keith...." I stammer. "I told him...about us...."

"I know, baby," he breathes and kisses the back of my hand again. "I saw the video, remember?"

I wince again. I hate to think of Keith watching that, but in a way, it fills me with relief. I don't have to explain anything to him. He already knows the worst.

"Is the rest of the crew okay?" I ask.

He shrugs. "Not really. Everyone is worried about you."

I don't know what to say to that, but right then, someone comes to the door of my hospital room. It's Jim Walker, the Chief of Police. "Hey, Keith, could I have a word with you in the hall?"

Keith kisses my hand again and leaves. I don't know what to do with myself, but I feel too crappy to move. How long will it take before I start feeling normal?

I have an IV hooked up to my arm, a bunch of cardiac leads stuck to my chest and sides, and an oxygen cannula wrapped around my face. It shoots oxygen up my nose.

I sink back onto the pillows. I feel like I could pass out again. Just having one simple conversation with Keith exhausts me. No wonder I've been unconscious for.....I don't even know how long I've been unconscious.

Keith comes back, sits down in the same place, and picks up my hand. "What's going on?" I ask.

"The Police want to take your statement now. They got everything on the video, but they need you to give a statement of your own about everything you remember. They want to make sure they catch any details in case you pass out again or your injuries affect your memory."

"I wouldn't worry about that. I remember everything."

"That's all the more reason for you to give your statement now. I'm going to get the officers, okay?"

I barely have the strength to nod. He leaves and comes back with Jim and a bunch of other cops. Most of them are plain-clothes detectives in business suits.

Jim goes through the usual introduction explaining why they want to get my statement right away. I can only nod and agree.

It doesn't take me long to go through the story. The whole attack only lasted a few minutes—from my perspective, at least. Who knows how much longer Damon kept kicking me after I blacked out.

"That's all I remember," I finally tell the detectives. "I only remember hitting the emergency call button on my phone and then I passed out."

"Did Mr. Cassidy make threats against you before this?" one of the detectives asked.

I try to shrug. "He made them all the time—and not just against me. He threatened Keith....."

I wave to Keith, but the same detective raises his hand. "Did Mr. Cassidy make any specific threats against you? I'm not asking if he threatened anyone else."

"That's what I'm telling you. He made threats all the time, but they were pretty vague—like he said he would make me pay or that I would regret it or that he would make me sorry."

"Sorry for what, specifically?" one of the other detectives asked. "What did he threaten you for?"

"For cheating on him. That was his big thing. He suspected me of cheating on him, but I never did. He imagined it all. That's why I told him about me and Keith—to make Damon understand that we were finally over for good." I frown at them. "Shouldn't you have all of this on the video?"

"That's why we're asking," Jim interjects. "We need to know what went on between you before the attack—what pattern of threats and violence he used before this. We can't see that on the video."

"He never acted this violently before. He slapped me around, but never anything like this."

"He said a few things on the video," the same male detective adds. "A few things about how you didn't deserve to live after what you did to him."

I turn away feeling sick. "I don't want to know."

"I think we have enough information anyway," Jim tells me. "We'll leave you to recover. We shouldn't need to question you any further after this. The next time you hear from us, we should have Mr. Cassidy in custody."

"Thank you. I never imagined he would go as far as this."

"Most people don't imagine someone could go as far as this until they do." He smiles at me and waves the detectives out of the room.

I let out a shaky sigh and sink into my pillows again. I really need to go back to sleep. I feel like hell.

Keith moves over to my side and sits down on the mattress again. He takes my hand and smiles at me, but right then, a scuffle breaks out in the hall.

Half of the detectives are still in the room. The rest gather in the hall where a bunch of uniformed officers stand guard.

I can't hear what any of them are talking about, but another voice echoes from out of sight. "Leila!! Leila!! Where are you?!"

Keith turns around and my every nerve stretches to the breaking point when I recognize Damon's voice.

I'm too injured to move, but Keith stands up and turns to face the door just as Damon storms down the hall yelling my name into every room. "Leila!! Leila!! Where is she? What did you do with her?!"

He makes it as far as the glass windows of my room. All the Police personnel move into his path to block his way and he goes ballistic. "LEILA!!"

"Simmer down, pal," Jim tells him, but Damon completely ignores him.

He turns to yell into my room next and Damon's face goes black when he sees Keith standing next to my bed. "What the hell is he doing in there?! You son of a bitch! You better get the hell away from her....!"

Damon lunges for the door and all the officers grab him to hold him back. Keith stiffens, but he doesn't move from my bedside.

Damon bellows curses loudly enough for the whole hospital to hear him. All the uniformed officers converge to restrain him, and when that doesn't work, Jim and the detectives join in.

Damon still manages to break their hold to make one last-ditch rush for my room door before all the officers pile on top of him and drag him to the floor. I lose sight of them, but the sounds of blows, curses, and enraged bellows drift from out of sight.

Keith remains planted next to my bed. He can see everything through the window. I don't want to see. Why does Damon have to make this so hard—for himself and everyone else?

After way too long, the officers all stand up, dust themselves off, and straighten their uniforms. Damon keeps yelling obscenities from the floor, but they must have cuffed him because I still can't see him.

The officers hold a quick conference and then some of the uniformed men drag Damon away still raving.

The rest of them stand around talking, filling out paperwork, and leaving in twos and threes. Another hour must pass before Jim finally comes into my room.

He's still breathing heavily when he says, "Sorry you had to see that....Well.....just to let you know.....Mr. Cassidy is now in custody."

Chapter 15: Keith

I pull up my truck to the curb and both Leila and I look through the windshield at her house. She shudders. "I don't think I can go back in there. I don't want to see....."

She trails off and I glance over at her. The swelling in her face has gone down considerably, but most of her face, head, neck, and body are still black and blue from so many bruises.

They're starting to change color after more than ten days in the hospital, but at least I can see the way she used to look. Her eyes aren't as puffy and her lips are back to their normal shape. It's the rest of her that still looks like she got run over by a truck.

"You don't have to go in there," I tell her. "I can take you to my place. You never have to set foot in that house again as long as you live if you don't want to."

She gulps. She won't even look at me. Her terrified eyes lock on the house—her house. That bastard Damon stole that from her, too. Now she'll never feel safe even in her own home.

I don't wait for her to answer. Now isn't the time for her to face that particular demon.

I shift my truck into gear and drive across town to my place. I cast a few flinty glances up and down the street and all around the parking lot before I go around to open Leila's door for her. If that twerp Damon shows up here, I want to be ready.

He's still in jail the last I heard, but he won't stay there forever. I don't know what I'll do if he does show up, but it won't be pretty.

I help her out and she slowly, painstakingly limps into the building. I keep a hold on her hand all the way, but I make sure to survey the surroundings just in case our boy decides to pull a fast one on us. I'll probably be looking over my shoulder for the rest of my life as long as he's still alive.

I get Leila into the elevator and we ride up to my floor. Neither of us says anything until we get inside the apartment. I double- and triple-lock the door just in case.

She hobbles into the living room, scans the furnishings just to make sure everything is still in the same place, and then goes into the bedroom.

She freezes on the threshold when she sees the suitcase sitting on the bed. "What's this?" she asks.

"I thought you might not want to stay at your place, so I brought some of your clothes and stuff over here so you'd be more comfortable. I didn't want you going over there if you didn't absolutely have to."

She looks up at me and her eyes glisten with emotion. Then she slumps onto the bed. "I'm sorry I'm not much good to you like this."

"What are you talking about? You're so much good to me like this." I sit down next to her on the bed and take her hand again. "You're here—in my apartment. What could be better than that? We're together. This will blow over eventually and our lives will go on. This won't last forever."

"I'm glad you think so."

"Hey! Don't talk like that." I lean in and kiss her on the side of the head. This is the first time I've dared to kiss her since that morning before she got attacked. "Everything will be okay. You'll see."

She looks up at me. I can't tell if she believes me, but now I'm certain of it. We're together. I won't let anything spoil this for me.

"Why don't you lie down for a while?" I tell her. "Are you hungry? I can make you something to eat....or drink."

"Um....thanks. That would be great."

"Breakfast, lunch, or dinner?" I ask.

Her head shoots up and she laughs. "It's two o'clock in the afternoon."

"That's why anything goes. Pick your poison."

She laughs a few more times and then winces. "Um....dinner, I guess."

"Good choice. Lie down and relax. Here's the remote for the TV...."

"Would you mind giving me my phone? I need to text my parents."

I get her phone out of her handbag. She's been obsessed with her phone ever since the attack—not that I blame her. She never really settles down unless she's holding it in her sweaty little hand.

It's a good thing she can still use it because her parents have been only slightly less obsessed about her condition ever since they got the news.

They wanted to fly out to Howe and stay with her, but she told them not to. I'm still not sure why. Maybe she feels ashamed of getting into an abusive relationship. I don't know.

I go to the kitchen and make a casserole dish of mac and cheese with bacon, ham, and broccoli. I serve it to her in bed while we catch up on the TV news.

"When are you going back to work?" she asks me after it ends.

"I'm not sure. I guess we'll just see how things go."

"You have to go back eventually," she tells me. "You can't just quit. *I* can't just quit."

"I'm on paid family emergency leave. I can take up to three months off if I need to."

She spins around and her mouth falls open. "You.....you did that—for me?"

"Actually, John was the one who did it. I also had almost six months of paid vacation time that I haven't used, so we're tacking that onto the total." I kiss the side of her head again. "You don't worry about me and work. Me and work have a mutual understanding and there is nothing in the world you can do to threaten that. Trust me."

She looks away. "I know. Believe me. I just don't want you to jeopardize anything because of me."

"I'm not. Now eat your broccoli. You need to build yourself up."

She laughs and settles back on the pillows. "Yes, dear."

I have to smirk at her. "I like the sound of that. Maybe I should invest in a French maid's outfit so you can watch me dust the apartment half-dressed."

She snorts and starts coughing. "I think I'll skip it."

I settle back and relax. I'm enjoying myself too much to care about work or anything else. Just these little exchanges of friendly banter remind me of the way things used to be. Now I know everything is going to be all right.

I don't care if she has to stay in my apartment for the rest of her life. In fact, I hope she does. I never want her to leave.

She finishes eating and I take her dishes back to the kitchen. I clean up, and when I get back to the bedroom, she's lying down with her eyes closed.

I tiptoe through the apartment turning off all the lights. I double- and triple-check the front door to make sure it's locked. Then I creep back to the bedroom, get undressed, and slip into bed next to her.

I let out a sigh of relief. I can finally rest, now that she's here with me.

I'm just about to go to sleep when she sighs, rolls over, and wraps her body around me the way she did that night she spent here with me.

She snuggles into my side and burrows her face into my neck. She smells different after being in the hospital for so long, but that will go back to normal soon, too.

I put my arms around her and experience another flood of happiness and almost painful emotion that she's finally here. She's finally mine. I don't have to doubt that any longer.

Her breathing lengthens and I let myself float again, but in a second, she slips her hand up the side of my face, threads her fingers into my beard, and turns my head toward her.

Before I even realize what she's going to do, she pulls out of my neck and starts kissing me as deeply and passionately as she ever did before. I don't want to hurt her, but she doesn't seem to feel the bruising in her face.

She heaves off the bed, and in a split second, she's all over me. She props herself on her elbow and kisses me with deep, open-mouthed kisses. Her fingers play in my hair and she massages the back of my neck before she goes back to combing my beard.

She leans a little closer and I feel the tension buzzing through her body. I hesitate to touch her—any of her. I don't know what to do with her. I thought she was too injured to do anything, but I must have been wrong about that.

She tips a little farther toward me. I expect her to roll on top of me, but after another minute, she falls down on the mattress next to me. She tries her best to keep a hold on my face so we can keep kissing, but she's too far away now.

"You're supposed to be resting, sweetheart," I tell her. "Doctor's orders."

"That sounds like *your* order." Her eyes drift open. She is definitely looking at me like that. "I don't remember the doctor saying anything about that."

"He didn't say it because he probably assumed, like I did, that you were too messed up to go there."

"Well, I'm not." She rears off the bed to kiss me and immediately falls back down, but there's no denying the look in her eyes. "I want you, Keith."

I have to have her when she looks at me like that. I roll onto my side and push myself onto my elbow. I fall into the depths of kissing her, but I still don't want to go too far.

She reacts the same way, circles her arms around my neck, and tries to pull me down on top of her. I am definitely not doing that. My weight could put her back in the hospital.

Well, maybe it wouldn't be that bad, but I don't want to chance it when I just got her home.

She rakes her fingers down my back, up the backs of my thighs, and tries to touch me everywhere. Her hands and the sensation of her digging her fingers into me starts to spiral me out of control. I have to pull it back before we go too far. I don't even know how far is too far.

I pry myself out of her grip, but when I see her eyes glazed with desire and smoky passion, I realize how much she needs this. She won't be able to relax if she doesn't.

"Are you sure you want to do this?" I ask.

"Yes!" she whispers. "I need you."

She tries to kiss me again, but now I'm in control. We're going to do this my way or not at all. I can't let her get carried away with herself.

I sit up in bed and take hold of the pajamas I brought for her to wear home from the hospital. She sits up so I can pull the shirt over her head and then lies down so I can slide her pants off.

She stretches out naked on my bed. Different colored bruises cover her whole body, including her stomach, breasts, arms, and thighs. The only parts of her that Damon left unscathed are her legs below the knees and her arms below the elbows.

Seeing her like this stiffens my resolve not to do anything to harm her any more than she already has been harmed. She has a long road to recovery in front of her. I don't want to make it longer.

I shift over onto my hands and knees, but I don't lower my weight on top of her. I stay there with a good eight inches between my body and hers.

I kiss her as deeply and tenderly as I want to, but I don't touch her.

She raises her hands and touches me all over my body. Her touch sends explosions through me, and eventually, she finds her way down to my package between my legs.

I groan when she starts stroking me. She teases me to rock hardness and then pulls me down between her legs.

She rubs my shaft in her wetness and writhes on the bed trying to get me to lower myself inside her, but I don't go any lower.

She drives me crazy when she looks into my eyes like that. I have to have her. I need her as much as she needs me, but nothing shakes my determination to do this right.

She keeps stroking me to send me out of my mind. I can't hold out any longer, so I pivot off her and lay down on my side next to her.

She gulps and grimaces when she sees me moving away from her, but now I can pull her toward me. I scoot closer to her on the bed, hook one elbow under her leg, and angle myself to enter her.

Her eyes float half-closed and she moans in perfect surrender when I glide in nice and slow and easy. She buckles onto my chest and I can hear from her noises that she's okay with this. She isn't feeling any pain—only rapture.

I kiss the top of her head and the same overpowering flood of love and bliss pulls me under the waves of one stroke after another. The sensation of her surrounding me and her head resting on my chest is the most perfect homecoming I could ask for.

I grip the back of her neck with my other hand and pick up the pace. She gasps and claws her fingertips into my shoulders, but she's still enjoying this.

She flexes her midsection to drill down on my thrusts and her muscles clench around me when I drive in to the hilt.

I need to see her. I need to look into her eyes when she gives herself to me like this—especially now. This means so much to me. I need to know it means the same thing to her.

I scoop up her neck and cup her chin to lift her face. Her eyes keep losing focus every time I plow in. She comes back to lucidity for a second when I pull out and then she succumbs again on the next wave.

I kiss her, but her lips don't respond. She gasps and moans too rapidly and her lips quiver as her excitement builds.

I want her to focus on me, but this somehow means so much more. She grasps at my arms and chest as her body erupts in volcanic energy. She clutches at me and her eyes plead when she manages to focus at all.

I love seeing her like this. I love how much she aches for it even when her body wants to let her down.

All at once, she screams and collapses again. She crunches over and her head hits my chest as tremors rock her all over. She slams herself down on me with unbelievable power and then freezes there as shudders take her.

I want so much more, but I can wait. I don't want to push her past her limit. She huddles on my chest whimpering and crying for a long time. Her body twitches all over and her muscles clench around my shaft as wave upon wave of climax sweeps her away.

She finally lets out a painful convulsion and I let go of her leg. I slip out of her and ease her onto her back, but she turns back to me right away.

Her face wrenches. I can't stand seeing her in distress, but I'm already powering down. I don't need to go any further—not tonight.

I roll onto my back, wrap my arm around her shoulders, and cradle her against me until her tremors die away completely. She lifts her face just enough to nuzzle into my neck and then she lies still.

Her body feels immaculate and warm and so, so inviting next to me. I've never been so happy not to get off with someone, but that's what this is all about.

My time will come when she feels stronger. I don't have to worry about that, and when it happens, look out.

Chapter 16: Keith

I wake up the next morning in the same position, blink extra hard to get the glue out of my eyes, and turn to see Leila watching me. "Um....hi."

She bursts into a huge grin. "Hi."

I frown at her. "How long have you been awake?"

"About an hour, I think."

"You should have woken me up."

"No way. You needed to sleep."

I look away. I don't know how she found out about me losing sleep over her in the hospital. Maybe she just put it together based on the way I was acting.

I drag myself out of bed and flinch when I see the clock. "Jesus! It's almost ten o'clock!"

"You said you were on emergency leave," she points out.

"I need to call John and check in with him. The whole crew was waiting for news about you getting out of the hospital. They said they might stop by your place. They'll have a canary if they get there and you aren't there."

I swing my legs over the side of the bed and fish my phone out of my pants pocket. I tap it to wake it up and freeze when I see a text from John already on it. *Stay home. Damon got out on bail this morning.*

"Is something wrong?" Leila asks.

I shove the phone at her and scramble to put on my pants. Then I pull open the closet. I push the doors all the way aside and take down a long, rectangular case from the top shelf.

"What are you doing?" she asks.

I lay the case on the floor, unlock both locks with the key on my keychain, and raise the lid. "If he's out on bail, there's only one place he'll go. When he finds out you aren't at your place, he'll come looking for you at the next most logical spot."

I take out my twelve-gauge shotgun and start shoving cartridges into the chamber. Leila watches in horror from the bed, but this is serious business. Having the door locked doesn't mean a thing.

I load the first shotgun and start on the second one before she snaps out of her trance. She gets out of bed on the other side, puts on her pajamas, and goes into the bathroom without a word.

The shower switches on, but I'm too busy loading my second shotgun. I take both guns into the living room and put the second one on the kitchen counter while I make a sweep of the apartment.

Damon isn't here in the first place, but I can't get my nerves to calm down.

I take my first gun over to the windows, survey the parking lot, the street, and the rest of town beyond the trees across the street. Then I take a look through my telescope, but I don't see Damon anywhere.

I go back into the bedroom. Leila has lifted her suitcase onto the bed and is taking out some normal clothes and getting dressed. "Are you hungry?" she asks me. "I'll make breakfast."

"Yeah, okay," I reply, but I barely hear her. I look out through the bedroom windows, check the bathroom, and then check the second bedroom.

I don't know much about Damon Cassidy, but I know he's a coward and a crafty bastard. When he does come, we won't see him until he lands on top of us. I need to be ready.

I keep making one circuit of the apartment after another. Leila goes into the kitchen and starts making pancakes. I recognize that she's making herself at home in my apartment like she plans to stay here forever, but I can't appreciate that. I'm too keyed up.

She finds a package of walnuts in the pantry and adds those to the batter. I really should tell her that walnuts in pancakes are my favorite, but I get distracted by a car pulling into the apartment building parking lot downstairs.

I check, but the driver and none of the passengers are Damon. It's a family with two small children. They enter the building and everything goes quiet outside.

I really need to calm down. Damon might take weeks to strike. I won't be able to stay this on edge the whole time.

I don't know when he'll strike. That's the problem. He might wait long enough for me to let my guard down. In fact, I'm certain he will.

I can just imagine the nightmare of Leila and I going on with our normal lives. We'll both go back to work and he could strike on one of her calls when I'm not around. The bastard might even orchestrate a call to lure her away from the firehouse where no one suspects him.

I shake those thoughts out of my head—or try to.

"Come eat your breakfast," she calls across the room.

I go back to the kitchen counter and sit down on one of the stools, but I make sure to keep my shotgun right next to my hand where I can grab it at a moment's notice.

She puts a plate of pancakes in front of me and the syrup bottle next to my elbow. Then she pours me a cup of freshly brewed coffee and adds milk and sugar just the way I like it.

I frown at her over my plate. "How do you know how I like my coffee?"

She makes a face at me. "We've worked together almost every day for years. I've seen you put milk and sugar in your coffee on every single shift. I would have to be pretty dim not to notice how you drink your coffee."

"Okay, good point."

She pours another dollop of batter into the pan to make some pancakes for herself. She smiles to herself while she works. She looks about as happy as I feel—or how I felt before I found out that Damon was out on bail.

I cut my pancakes with the edge of my fork and put some in my mouth. They taste fantastic. I am definitely going to have to recruit this woman to cook for me more often—but that's the plan, isn't it?

I take a drink of my coffee and pick up my fork again when someone pounds their fist on the apartment door. "Leila!!" Damon bellows out in the hall. "Leila—I know you're in there!"

I snatch my shotgun and tip over my stool hustling to the door. He slams his fist on it a bunch more times and then the doorknob rattles when he tries to turn it.

"Get the hell out of here, man!" I yell through the door. "You aren't welcome here! You and Leila are finished and you're in violation of your restraining order." I nod to Leila and make a silent hand gesture of a phone.

She nods back, races to the bedroom, and comes back with her phone. She taps frantically on the screen and holds the phone to her ear, but I don't hear what she says to the operator on the other end.

Damon bangs his fist again. "Let me talk to Leila! I just want to talk to her! You can understand that, can't you?"

"You were talking to her when you beat her up and put her in the hospital!" I yell back. "You had your chance. You won't ever talk to her again!"

He doesn't answer. Everything goes too quiet out in the hall.

I rotate away from the wall, shoulder my shotgun, and aim it at the door. If he's standing outside, one shot will put him down for good.

He doesn't make a sound out there. I don't even hear him walk away. I wait and the tense, nerve-racking minutes tick past. Is he even still out there?

Leila stands at the other end of the kitchen counter by the fridge. She presses her phone to her ear, but she isn't talking to anyone anymore.

I hold my breath to listen, but I still don't hear anything. After what seems like forever, I can't stand the suspense anymore.

I ease over to the door and lower my eye to the peephole. Damon is still standing out there. From what I can see, he isn't doing anything other than just standing there. What is he up to?

I take my eye away from the peephole and get ready to step back to hold the door at gunpoint again. At that moment, before I can move, an almighty blast smashes the door in. I don't see anything out in the hall that could have caused that.

The door flies inward with unstoppable force, crashes into me, and sends me staggering. Before I even realize what's happening, Damon storms into the apartment, raises a handgun, and fires straight at my head.

Another crushing blow slams into my head and I pinwheel out of the way. Leila screams, but I'm already falling backward onto the floor. None of my limbs work well enough to break my fall.

I hit the floor hard with my eyes fixed wide open. I can't even blink or shut them. I fall on my back with my head turned sideways. I can see the whole living room and kitchen. Nothing stops me from seeing Damon stalk into my apartment gripping the gun in his hand.

He kicks my shotgun away and stands over me holding me at gun-point—as if I might be able to move enough to threaten him.

He sneers down into my face. "Nice try—pal. Better luck next time."

My brain is so dulled and foggy that I can't even get mad at him. I stare up at him in stunned shock. I understand the words, but they don't make the connection in my mind.

I can't stop him from threatening Leila, but not even thinking that is enough to trigger me to get mad or worried for her safety. I can only lie here and stare as he turns away and scans the room.

He doesn't do anything for a second. Silence throbs through the apartment. He doesn't leave to go hurt Leila. Will he hurt her right in front of me? Is that his plan?

His eyebrows jerk together in the middle and he cocks his head to listen. Nothing. Not a sound disturbs that deep, awful silence. Did something happen to Leila? Where is she? I can't see or hear her at all and neither can Damon.

He takes one step away from me, angles his head from one side to another, and sweeps his gun across the living room and kitchen. "Leila? Come on out, sweetie. I don't want to hurt you."

She doesn't come out and she doesn't make a sound, wherever she's hiding. I don't understand it. She was just here two seconds ago. She was standing right over there by the fridge when he broke in here.

He walks deeper into the apartment toward the living room and scowls toward the hall leading to the bedroom. Did she escape down there when he burst in?

I can see him thinking the same thing. He walks that way and calls down the hall. "Leila? You can't hide from me. I'll find you either way. Make it easier on yourself and just come out. We can work this out."

He stops at the threshold where the hall branches off the living room. He turns his ear toward the bedroom, but when he doesn't hear anything, he comes back toward me.

He frowns even more deeply. He's as puzzled as I am about where she is and where she went. Did she call 911? Are the Police and fire crew on the way right now?

He stops next to me like we might be friends sharing the same problem. We're definitely thinking the same things. I just can't move to go look for her as badly as I want to.

Now I'm really getting worried and not because this nutcase is standing over me holding the gun he used to shoot me in the head.

He swivels in all directions, passes the gun across the kitchen again, and then across the living room. He grits his teeth when he still doesn't see or hear her.

He takes a few steps toward the apartment door. It stands wide open to the hall outside.

He looks out into the hall and turns back into the apartment. I can see him about to walk over to me again when Leila springs out from behind the kitchen counter. She must have been hiding there all along. That explains why he didn't see her.

She attacks him so fast I can only stare in amazement. She doesn't look weak or injured or exhausted at all.

She lunges for Damon and swings the broom handle downward with a vicious stroke. It cracks across his wrist and strips the gun out of his hand. The gun hits the floor with a crash and Damon turns on her bellowing in pain and rage.

There's no stopping her now. She recovers instantly, winds back the broom handle, and delivers a punishing blow right across his face. He buckles on the spot and she springs over him to my side.

She drops the broom and completely ignores him while she bends over me. She takes a split second to kick the gun across the floor. Then she gets right in front of my eyes talking fast. "Hold on, Keith! You're gonna be all right. I'm gonna take care of you. Don't worry. We're gonna get you to the hospital. Everything is gonna be okay."

She doesn't flinch when she says it and I don't hear a trace of a quaver in her voice. She's back. She switches into paramedic mode and I feel her touching my head and body, but the sensation comes from far away.

She dives away and comes back pressing her phone to her ear. "My name is Leila Cunningham. I'm a paramedic with Howe County Fire Department. We need Police, Fire, and EMS on scene at 1566 Cambridge Terrace, Apartment 518. We have one man with a gunshot wound to the head and another with blunt-force trauma to his face. Yes, Ma'am. I know. The gunshot victim is still conscious and alert, but his motor functions are impaired. I don't know about the other guy. I haven't assessed him yet."

She moves the phone away from her mouth, leans forward, and positions herself in front of my face so I can't see anything but her. "You're going to be okay, Keith. Just hold on until the crew gets here. We're gonna get you out of here."

I believe her. She's in battle mode and there's no stopping her when she gets like this.

She keeps shooting information to the emergency dispatcher on the other end of the line....and then I hear sirens in the distance.

Leila hangs up and does a few more things to me, but I can't keep track of what she's doing. Things get a little fuzzy, and the next time my vision clears, dozens of people pack my apartment.

Leila, Naomi, Chris, and Jessie all work on me at once and I have an oxygen mask over my face. Danny, Billy, Ellis, and Caleb surround me and I feel their hands immobilizing me.

Danny kneels by my head holding me still while Chris fits a neck collar around my neck. They slide me onto a backboard and then lift me onto a gurney.

Leila leans in again. "We're taking you to the hospital, Keith. I'm right here. I'll be right here with you all the way."

I feel her touch my hand. I want to tell her that I love her. I should have said it last night. I should have said it so many times and now I can't say anything, not even to thank her for helping me.

The gurney starts moving, but she stays right there by my side all the way to the elevator, all the way out of the building, all the way into the ambulance, and all the way to the hospital.

She gives orders to the guys on where to move the gurney and she fires off orders to the other paramedics about which drugs to give me.

Then she gives orders to the medical staff—right up until the moment when they wheel me into surgery.

She bends down and kisses me on the mouth in front of everyone—the fire crew and the medical team. "The team is going to anesthetize you now, Keith, but I'll be right here waiting for you when you come out. I love you. You're going to be all right, and when you get out, everything will go back to the way it was. Damon is dead, so we'll never have to worry about him ever again."

She says it so casually without a hint of emotion. She killed him with that blow to his face and she doesn't even care.

I don't care, either. She loves me and Damon is gone. He's out of our lives forever. I never have to look over my shoulder again and as soon as I recover from this, she's all mine. We'll go home and we'll be together from now on.

God, I want to touch her right now! I want to hold her and tell her how much I love her, but I can't do that.

Never mind. I'll tell her when I get out of surgery. I'm going to make it. I know that now. She's so certain that I have no choice but to believe it, too.

She's a paramedic. She can see my condition so much better than I can. If she's so certain I'm going to be fine, I believe her.

Her certainty makes me feel so much better. I can just relax and concentrate on recovering.

The next minute, the medical team wheels me through a set of swinging doors. I lose sight of her, the fire crew, and everyone else I know.

Before I can begin to freak out about that, someone in a mask puts something over my face and I pass out completely.

Chapter 17: Keith

I wake up and groan. My head feels like someone hit me with a hammer—because they did.

My hand flies to my head and I feel a huge bandage wrapped around my skull. The sunshine coming through the window makes my head hurt even more. Even thinking hurts.

Leila comes over to sit on the edge of my bed. "Hey, big guy," she murmurs and rests her hand on my chest through the blankets. "You're okay. You came through the surgery just fine."

"What happened?" I croak. "I mean, I remember what happened, but.....how bad was the gunshot?"

"It wasn't that bad," she tells me. "I mean, you getting shot in the head wasn't great, but it could have been a lot worse. The bullet hit you on the outside of your eyebrow and glanced off. It fractured your skull, but it didn't cause any brain damage. You're going to make a full recovery. You're just going to have a splitting headache for a while."

"Great," I growl and then pull myself together to look up at her.

She looks perfectly fine because she is. She still has all the bruising on her face from Damon's attack, but other than that, she's totally unharmed.

"Are you okay?" I ask. "I mean....you said before I went into surgery that Damon was dead."

"Yeah. I guess I hit him harder than I realized. I wasn't thinking about anything except hitting him as hard as I possibly could. I wanted to put him down. I didn't think about anything else."

"Are you okay—about that, I mean?" I clasp her hand. "Thank you. I can't thank you enough for saving me. I owe you one for that."

She snickers. "You can put it on my tab for all the times you've saved me."

"I mean it. Are you okay? I'm sorry—about Damon. That must be hard on you."

"I'm okay," she replies and I can see that she is. She's more than okay. She's perfect. "I don't really think about it, to be honest. I had to give a report to the Police Department about the whole incident and they're ruling it as self-defense. The Police have security camera footage from the hall of your apartment building. There was a camera near the elevator that caught him blowing your door in and then there was another camera right outside your door. It was pointed into the apartment the whole time he was inside. It caught everything—him shooting you and me hitting him—so no one disputes what happened."

I sigh and lean back on the pillows. "Are you sure you're okay with it? I know he meant a lot to you."

She shrugs. "I'm fine with it. I did what I had to do to save both of us. There's no question in my mind that he was going to kill me and then he probably would have finished you off, too. I couldn't let that happen."

"Come here." I scoop my hand behind her head and pull her in to kiss her. I don't ever want to let go of her again.

The minute my lips touch hers, movement distracts me from the other side of the bed. John walks over to me and squeezes the lower part of my leg through the blanket. Danny stands behind him leaning against the windowsill, but they're both smiling at me.

"We'll get out of here and leave you two alone," John tells me.

"Have you two been standing there this whole time?" I demand. "Why didn't you say something?"

"We didn't want to interrupt," Danny tells me. "She wasn't saying anything we wouldn't have said."

I groan and rub my head again, but that only makes it hurt more. "You guys should have said."

"Naw," John counters. "We'll get out of your hair. We just wanted to make sure you were all right, but you'll be in good hands as long as Leila's here. The whole crew is waiting downstairs to hear when you wake up."

"The *whole* crew?" I ask.

"Yep," Danny replies. "Even crews who are on duty. They can respond to calls as easily from here as they can from the station."

I shut my eyes. I don't want to think about the entire fire crew hanging out in the hospital because of me. My throat tightens. I never thought......

I turn away and try not to make it too obvious when I gulp down the lump in my throat. I never thought I meant that much to them. I don't know why I'm surprised, but I am.

John gives my leg one more squeeze. "It's good to have you back, brother. Take all the time you need." He nods to Leila. "Call me if anything happens."

"Okay," she replies and I can tell by the way she smiles at both him and Danny that it's all over. She's part of the family now which means Ellen knows, too.

None of them will ever question me being with Leila. We're to-gether—as together as John and Ellen are. It all happened so fast, but it makes such perfect sense.

He and Danny leave and I immediately turn to Leila. "Listen....I love you. I wanted to tell you before I went into surgery....but I couldn't."

She smiles even more broadly and her eyes glisten with happiness. "I know. Don't worry. I know."

She lets her hand fall against my cheek and her fingers thread into my beard when she leans forward to kiss me.

I put my arms around her and pull her down on top of me. She settles down on the bed and then stretches out next to me.

I shut my eyes, but I can only see that moment when she attacked Damon with the broom handle. I'll never forget that as long as I live. She's a true hero. She saved my life and her own. There's no doubt about that.

I turn my head just enough to kiss her on the forehead. As long as I keep my eyes closed, I can fool myself that I'm not in the hospital. I'm in my own bedroom—our bedroom. I'm in my own bed holding her before we both fall asleep.

Thinking that helps me relax the rest of the way. I must have fallen asleep for real, because I wake up later and the windows are dark. It's nighttime now.

Leila sits on a chair by the window doing something on her phone. No one else is here.

I take a breath and she looks up. She smiles at me, but right then, John walks in with the whole fire crew behind him. More and more people stream in. They have to crowd together to make room for everyone.

"Hey, he's awake!" Ellis chirps. "Welcome back from the Beyond, pal."

"Beyond what?" I growl and laughter breaks out among the others.

"Beyond belief," Billy replies. "You got one hell of a hard head, man."

"But we already knew that, right?" Caleb adds.

I groan and try to sit up, but my head hurts too much and I have to lie back down. "If you came here to gloat, you can take that crap straight back to the firehouse. You can make all the jokes you want at my expense as long as you do it there and not here."

"Oh, we will," Danny replies. "Don't you worry about that."

I glare at him, but he only grins at me. This playful teasing is just the way we show affection for each other. He'll always be my kid brother even though he's one of the best firefighters on the crew—right after me, of course.

We always shoot insults back and forth where I pretend to hate him. I should change that. I should show him how much he means to me, but from the way he's smiling at me, it looks like he already knows.

One glance around the crew tells me they all already know how much they mean to me and I can see how much I mean to them. They wouldn't be here if they didn't care.

I can't tell Danny I love him in front of the whole crew. They would all have a field day with that and he would be the first to turn it into a joke. I'll have to save it for when we're in private.

I can't put it off, though. I need to get that done, especially if I'm going to be getting shot in the head and putting my life on the line every day at work.

I've been doing that for years, but it took this gunshot wound to really make me see it. I won't live forever, especially not in this job.

I need to say those things to the people who mean the most to me. I need to say them while I still have a chance. I might not get another one next time—and there will be a next time. There's always a next time.

Chapter 18: Leila

I slam my car door in the firehouse parking lot, take a deep breath, and tug my jacket into place. I'm not wearing my uniform even though I've already been back at work for a week.

I check my appearance in the car window. The colors from my bruises are even more faded now, but they're still there. At least I look slightly normal.

Today is my day off and I'm wearing casual clothes, but I can't remember ever feeling this nervous about going into the firehouse.

I can't let myself back out, so I muster up my courage and walk into the garage. Everyone is upstairs in the break room, so I go upstairs and turn off to John's office. The door stands open.

I walk in and he looks up from his computer. "Hi," I greet him.

"Hi. Shouldn't you be at the hospital? Today's the big day. You're taking Keith home, right?"

"I'm on my way there now. I needed to talk to you first."

He turns the rest of the way around. "What about? Is anything wrong with Keith?"

"No, nothing's wrong with Keith. That's what I wanted to talk to you about. I'm taking Keith home from the hospital."

He hesitates and a slight frown pinches his eyebrows in the center. "Uh....yeah? And?"

"And....I'm staying there. I'm moving in with Keith. That's what I'm telling you. When I get him home, I'm staying at his apartment. I won't be going back to my place."

John waits for me to say something else. "Yeah?"

I wait for *him* to say something else. "So.....I'm moving in with him."

"I know. Is that all you wanted to tell me?"

I blink and then my eyes widened. "You...you knew?"

"Uh....yeah? Wasn't that the plan all along—you two being together?" He frowns again and then his eyes widen. "Did you think I would object or something?"

"Well....yeah. I mean......" I don't know what to say. "I thought....I don't know what I thought. I thought you would want to have some kind of father-daughter talk about me treating Keith right.....or I guess in this case, a big-brother talk. I don't know. I didn't think you would just......you know.....be so okay with it."

He makes a face and pushes some of his papers away. "Please. You two were made for each other and I'm not the only one who thinks so. If you didn't move in with him now, you would do it soon, but since he's still recovering, it makes sense for you to move in with him now."

"So.....you're okay with it?"

"Will you stop that? Of course I'm okay with it. You two are grown adults. You can make your own decisions, and even if you couldn't, I would never have any objection to you and Keith." He snorts. "Please."

"Oh. Okay. So....is Danny okay with it?"

He jerks forward and puts his elbows on the desk. "Will you get the hell out of here? Everyone is okay with it. Just go. Take Keith home from the hospital and then come back here for your shift. We all have work to do here."

He half-smirks, half-glares at me on my way out the door. That conversation so did not go the way I expected. In hindsight, I don't know what I expected.

John is Keith's older brother, but John is really like a father figure to all of us and I know Keith thinks of him that way. I don't think either of us would be able to go through with this relationship if John really did object—or we would at least have to rethink it.

I can't imagine why John would object, but I just wouldn't feel right about going any further with Keith without John's approval.

For some reason, I tend to think of John as something like my dad. I rely on him to keep track of my best interest as well as Keith's and everyone else's. That's John's role in all our lives.

If he thought there was a problem with me and Keith getting together, I would have to accept John's assessment. I would at least have to consider it and follow his recommendations. I know Keith feels that way, too.

I get in my car and drive to Keith's apartment where I park my car and get into his pickup. I drive it to the hospital and park as close to the entrance as possible before I go upstairs to his room.

I find him sitting on the edge of the bed in his sweatpants and a ragged hoodie I fished out of his closet. At least he's comfortable in his own clothes.

He looks different with half of his hair shaved off, but it makes him look even more grunge than he did before.

A wicked gash covers half his skull. It cuts from his forehead above his eyebrow and backward over his ear to a spot on the back of his head. He's going to carry that scar for life.

I pull the duffel bag with his clothes and personal effects out from under the bed. We've already packed up his stuff so he'll be ready to go as soon as the medical staff releases him.

I unzip the duffel bag and start collecting his medications, tooth-brush, post-op instructions, and phone from the bedside table. "Did you remember to get that mystery book you've been reading?" I ask.

"It's in there under my jeans. Don't forget that bag of candy in the cabinet."

He points to the cabinet under the bedside table. I raise my eye-brows at him. "Candy? You've been eating candy in the hospital?"

He makes a face. "Oakleigh brought it for me to cheer me up. It's unopened. Trust me."

I open the cabinet and take out a sealed bag of individually wrapped toffees. I grin at it. "That's really sweet."

"It's too bad I can't give them back to her. She's the only kid I know."

"You could leave them out in a bowl at the next firehouse barbecue. The kids will eat them then."

"Good idea." He stuffs them into the duffel bag.

We both go back to organizing his stuff when a nurse comes in pushing a wheelchair. "You've been released so you can go home now. Just shift over into this wheelchair and I'll take you downstairs."

He glares at her. "I don't need a damn wheelchair. I can walk out on my own. I'm not that weak and I'm not going to live in a nursing home."

"It's hospital policy. Everyone has to leave in a wheelchair." She gives him a giant smile. "Sorry. You can show everyone how tough you are as soon as you leave hospital property."

He growls under his breath, but he spares himself the effort of arguing with her. He cranes his weight off the bed, pivots, and sits down heavily in the wheelchair.

He glares at everyone and everything while she wheels him to the elevator, down to the lobby, and out to the truck. I carry the duffel bag and heave it into the back.

"Can I get out now?" he snarls when she locks the brakes by the passenger door.

"Yes, you're all set to go."

"You're sure, now?" he sneers. "Are you sure you won't have to pay an extra insurance premium if I stand on my own two feet? I wouldn't want to cause the hospital corporation any undue financial hardship or anything like that."

She laughs out loud and makes the mistake of trying to take his arm to help him stand up. He bares his teeth at her, yanks his arm out of her grasp, and pushes himself out of the chair.

He still moves slowly and he gasps in pain when he finally settles into the passenger seat. I smile at the nurse while she unlocks the wheels and turns the wheelchair away. "Thanks," I tell her.

"Have a quick recovery," she calls over her shoulder. "Good luck."

I get behind the wheel and smile over at Keith. He's already acting happier and more relaxed, now that she's gone.

I drive back to the apartment building, park, and take out the duffel bag while he gets out of the truck. He walks into the building just fine and rides the elevator up to the fifth floor.

I unlock the door for him to enter. I've spent the last two days cleaning the apartment, scrubbing all the blood stains off the floor, and getting the door repaired.

Before he crosses the threshold, he pauses there and looks up at the hall ceiling. A perfectly round, semi-circular dome of tinted plastic covers the security camera. We can't see the camera through the dome, but it's there. It keeps the whole hall under surveillance.

"You okay?" I ask.

"It's weird," he mutters. "I never even noticed it before."

"I didn't notice it, either, but it was a godsend. Jim Walker showed me the footage and the camera caught everything—and I mean literally everything."

Keith frowns at the camera and then turns to enter the apartment. I shut the door behind us.

Keith doesn't exactly shuffle his feet, but he doesn't move as energetically as he used to. He walks straight to the couch, sits, and scoots down to rest his head against the back. He shuts his eyes and sighs.

"Can I get you anything?" I ask. "Do you want to go lie down for a while?"

"No," he snaps. "I've been lying on my back for three weeks. I don't want to lie down ever again."

I laugh and he opens his eyes to look up at me.

"Come here and sit down next to me," he tells me. "I missed you."

I sit down next to him and pillow my head on his shoulder. He puts his arm around me and kisses the top of my head.

I don't remind him that I've been right next to him all day and every night ever since he got shot. I missed him, too. I missed this—being with him here—us being together as a couple. Our lives have been on hold while he's been hospitalized.

He raises his hand, cups my chin, and tips my head up so he can kiss me. I lean into him and rest my hand on his chest, but I don't want to do too much. I don't want to hurt him any more than he already has been hurt.

He escalates faster than I expected. He prods my mouth open, and before I think to say anything, he scoops his hands under my armpits and lifts me to sit sideways on his lap.

He wraps one arm around my waist and his other hand falls on my breasts. He massages them and squeezes and twists and teases while we kiss. I moan as the excitement builds.

He breaks off my mouth and dives for my chest. He gives me a few soft bites through my shirt and makes me gasp.

My hand flies to his head and I wake up when I touch the shaved side of his scalp. "Are you sure you should be doing this? Aaaahh! Keith......!"

He raises his head one more time and snatches a kiss from my mouth. "Of course I should be doing this. Do you know how long I've been waiting for this?"

He goes back to kissing me ravenously. He slides his hand between my thighs, and in a second, he works his way up to squeeze me between my legs.

I groan as ecstasy blasts me into outer space, but right then, a rush of heat pulses to his crotch. His package digs into me through his sweats, and as soon as it happens, he winces and collapses back on the couch.

His hand flies to his head and he presses his wrist to his eyebrow. "Aarrgh!"

I sit back on his lap and pet his cheeks while he grimaces in pain. "Maybe you should take it easy for a while—at least until you start feeling better."

"I don't want to take it easy for a while! I've been going crazy in the hospital with you right next to me. That bastard Damon! If he was here, I would kill him a second time."

I have to laugh. "Don't do that. Just concentrate on getting better. Your head will recover. Just give yourself some time."

"To hell with that." He looks up, wraps his arms around me, and goes back to kissing me, but we both take it much slower this time.

I can tell he wants to pick up the pace. He wants to do everything right now, but his body lets him down.

That's okay. He'll get better and everything else about our relationship will come back along with his strength.

Chapter 19: Keith

I walk into the firehouse garage to find the crew standing around. "Hey! Looking good, champ!" Caleb calls out.

The rest of the crew stops their conversation to greet me. Billy gives me a high-five and the paramedics hug me.

Leila's already here. She beams at me from across the circle, but she doesn't step out of place or say anything. This is all me. It's my first day back to work and it's about damn time.

Billy points to my scar. "You're really gonna scare the patients with that."

"As if they aren't scared enough already," Danny adds.

I ignore him. We've had our little talk, but no one needs to know about that, not even Leila. What Danny and I said to each other is just between him and me. Now we can go back to our old way of making fun of each other.

My hair has grown back to its normal length, but the scar still shows up. My hair covers the section of scar on the back of my head, but the part on my forehead stands out for all the world to see.

It disappears in a stark white line running into my hair, but I don't care what I look like. It's a badge of honor and the rest of the crew treats it that way, too.

They shoot their usual jokes back and forth, but they forget all about me and start cracking wise about their latest calls. The crew treats my presence as if me being here is the most normal thing in the world.

After a few minutes, John comes downstairs and sees us standing around. "Aren't you doing your checklists? What's the holdup?"

Danny snaps to attention and gives his best military salute. "Yes, Sir!"

The others laugh and we head for the trucks. I'm grateful to John for not mentioning me being here at all. I'm part of the scenery again—which is the way I like it.

We start doing our checks and I climb into the cab to go over the recent logbook entries. Chris and Leila sit in their seat in the back going through their kits, drugs, and medical supplies.

"Do you need any Xanax to improve your mood, Keith?" Chris teases. "I have some here if you get too anxious on your first call."

"Shut up!" I growl over my shoulder and Leila laughs.

"Did you hear about John's newest hire?" she asks me. "The poor guy had a panic attack on a call and left the scene before we even finished extricating the patient. We didn't see him again and it turns out that he hitchhiked back to the station, got in his car, and left town without telling anyone. We haven't seen him since."

I spin around and put my arm across the seat to stare at her. "No way! He didn't!"

She nods and smirks at me. "That's seven failures so far."

Chris shuffles some sterile packaging in her drug kit. "Maybe I should ask John if he needs some Xanax. He lost a few patches of hair when he was going through the last stack of resumes for new applicants."

"Wow," I exclaim. "That's really bad. Are we really that hard to get along with?"

"I really thought that last guy was going to make it, too," Chris remarks. "He was laughing and talking to everyone before the call. He said he really liked the friendly atmosphere around the station. He said he's never seen a warmer, more welcoming crew. He even said he could see himself working here forever."

"Then we got the call and it all went sideways," Leila finishes. "John thinks the dude might have faked his resume and didn't have nearly as much experience as he pretended to."

"Or none at all," Chris adds.

"Man!" I turn back around in the seat and go back to rifling the logbook. "Well, that will definitely not happen to me, so you ladies can stop crossing your fingers."

They both laugh, and right then, Billy opens the rear passenger door and climbs up to put an extra self-contained breathing mask into the locker under the seat. "What's so funny up here?!" he growls in a fake threatening voice. "You kids are supposed to be working, not socializing on the clock."

"Go on and rat us out to the teacher," Chris tells him.

He grins at her and opens his mouth to answer when the fire alarm goes off. "Don't forget your Xanax, Keith!" Chris yells and laughs again.

I jump out of the truck, scramble into my turnouts, and jump back in to fire up the engine. The rest of the crew does the same thing, but the two paramedics are already in place.

They slam their doors and squirm into their turnouts while I pull the truck out onto the street.

We drive across town to the scene of a three-car wreck on the highway. Police officers surround the scene and direct traffic away. They've already set up cones to give us plenty of space to work.

The crew tumbles out to extricate the patients, and a second later, the ladder truck, two more ambulances, and John's support pickup arrive to help us.

Leila, Chris, Billy, Danny, and I end up working on one of the cars. There are three passengers and both the driver and the woman in the front passenger seat are out cold with blood running down their faces.

The woman in the back seat screams hysterically at me. She's bloody, too, and frantically yanks at her seat belt. "I can't get it off! Get this thing off me! Get me out of here! You have to get me out of here!"

I lean in through the door and try to reason with her. "I'll get you out! Just try to stay calm. Are you injured anywhere?"

"GET ME OUT OF HERE!!" she shrieks in my face. "I HAVE TO GET OUT OF HERE!!"

"Is she injured anywhere?!" Leila yells at me from the front seat.

I glance in her direction. She and Danny are working to extricate the driver while Chris and Billy work on the other passenger.

"Check her legs!" Leila tells me.

I do a quick sweep of my patient's legs while she screeches in my ear about how she can't undo the damn seatbelt. If I didn't have as much experience as I do on calls just like this, I would definitely be freaking out and leaving town about now.

"She looks all right!" I yell back to Leila. "She just has a head injury!"

"She's walking wounded!" Leila tells me. "Send her back to the ambulance crews."

I pull out my seatbelt tool and slice through the seatbelt easily. "Everything's going to be all right!" I tell the patient. "We're getting you out!"

She flounders trying to get out of the car and I guide her past the piles of broken glass. She stands up easily and pants with sobs as soon as I get her out of the car.

"Come over here to the ambulances," I tell her and steer her by the arm. "The paramedics will take a look at your head and transport you to the hospital. This way. That's right. Everything's going to be all right."

She whimpers a few more times and then grabs my arm. "Thank you so much! Thank you so much! You're an angel!"

"Okay," I mutter. "I'm just doing my job. You'll be okay. Here you g o."

I hand her off to Brooke, who smiles at me when she hears the woman call me an angel. Female patients calling me that has become a big joke around the firehouse. This woman doesn't even see my scar. It definitely doesn't frighten her.

I hustle back to the car and get busy helping Danny and Leila load the driver onto a backboard and gurney. Jessie and Naomi transport him straight to the hospital.

Brooke, Drew, and George are up to their armpits in more patients who aren't as critical. They sit on blankets on the pavement while the three medics go from one person to another triaging them as quickly as possible for priority transport.

By the time Leila, Danny, and I get back to the car, Chris and Billy are ready to extricate the other passenger. She's the last patient out. It's time to pack up and head for the station.

Billy drives the rescue truck back, which leaves more than enough time for Chris and Leila to tell the rest of the guys about my latest patient calling me an angel.

I put up with it the way I usually do. I can't begrudge the crew for getting a laugh at my expense. They have to get their jollies somewhere and I've been gone too long already. The crew has to make up for lost time.

I catch Leila laughing with the others, but the vibe on the crew is exactly the same as it was before she and I got together. John is right. Nothing has changed.

I get out when we pull up to the station. I enter the garage first and direct Billy to back the truck into place. Then everyone unloads and it's all about restocking and telling each other about our patients.

"And then Leila told me to spread the woman's legs wider apart so we could put the traction splint between them," Danny is saying. "I swear I died!"

"You seem alive enough to me," Billy remarks. "If you died, shouldn't you be at the morgue now?"

"You know what I mean!" Danny counters. "She told me to spread the woman's legs......"

He breaks off and a chill falls over the crew when John comes downstairs with Jim Walker and four of the plain-clothes detectives who questioned Leila about Damon's attack.

I freeze. Leila freezes. The whole crew freezes.

John waves to me. "These gentlemen want to ask you some questions about Damon Cassidy." He glances at Leila. "Both of you."

"What about him?" I fire back. "You have the security camera footage. You already know what happened."

"The Department is holding an inquiry into his death....." Jim begins.

"Why?" Leila interrupts. "You told me it was self-defense and you wouldn't be pressing any charges."

"We aren't pressing any charges," he replies. "This is simply a fact-finding investigation."

"You have all the facts," I tell him. "We've already told you everything we know."

"We need to question you about Damon's behavior before the event." Jim turns to survey the rest of the crew. "In fact, we should probably go through it with the rest of you, too."

"We can't tell you anything," Chris points out. "We weren't there for either attack."

"I'm talking about before that. I understand from Ms. Cunningham's and Mr. Brewer's statements that Mr. Cassidy acted violently and made threats in public—in the presence of all of you. Isn't that correct?"

The rest of my crewmates exchange glances and shuffle their feet. "Yeah, he did," Billy mutters.

"Then we need to take all your witness statements…..if you aren't too busy."

One glance at John tells all of us loud and clear that he's just fine with us giving our statements during our shift—as in right this very minute. Fantastic. I can't wait.

Jim makes eye contact with me and waves me toward the stairs. "If you wouldn't mind….."

I grit my teeth, bow my head, and head upstairs. Jim goes in front with two detectives following behind me. Now I really feel like I'm on my way to the firing squad.

Things take a turn for the horrific when we walk into John's office. He doesn't come with us. Jim sits down in John's chair and one of the detectives stands next to him. The other detective stands off to the side.

Jim folds his hands together on the desk and leans forward. "Take a seat, Keith."

I don't move. I stay standing. I don't want these guys to pretend they aren't interrogating me when they obviously are.

Jim waits, but when I don't sit down, he spreads his fingers before lacing them together again. "Right, well, what can you tell us about Damon's behavior before he shot you?"

"What are you talking about?" I counter. "He broke into Leila's house and destroyed her before he shot me. What the hell are you asking me this for? You already know what he did before he shot me."

"Did you have any advanced warning that he was going to try to kill you and Leila?" the detective to my right asks.

I spin around to confront him. "You mean besides all the times he said he was going to put me down and make me pay and that I would be sorry for having anything to do with her? Is that what you mean by advanced warning? That sounds pretty clear to me, don't you think?"

"You stated in previous reports that you got a text from your brother John the morning of the assault," the other detective interjects from Jim's side. "You stated that John alerted you that Damon was out on bail and John told you to stay home."

I jerk around the other way to face him. Are they doing this on purpose to throw me off my game? "That's right. So what?"

"You also stated that you started loading your weapons right after you got that text," the other detective adds. "You stated that you surveyed the surroundings outside the apartment because you anticipated Damon coming after Leila again. You stated that he knew by then that you two were involved and that she'd spent the night at your apartment."

"Yeah? So? He already put her in the hospital for getting involved with me. What was I supposed to do—wait for him to come and kill her?"

"What made you think he was coming to kill her?" Jim asks. "That's what we want to know. What made you think he would try to kill either of you?"

I shrug. I shouldn't let these guys rattle me or let them see me rattled, but it's too late. I already am. "I had no idea what he would do, but I sure as hell didn't plan to stand around waiting to find out."

"Did you see when you looked through the peephole that he had a gun?" the detective to my right asks.

I don't turn this time. I'm sick of jumping every time one of them talks to me. "No. I didn't see that he had a gun. I already told you in my statement that I didn't see him doing anything threatening in the hall."

"He planted explosives on either side of your door," the detective in front of me says. "That's how he blew it open. Did you see any of that?"

"No! How many times do I have to say it?"

"So you had no way of knowing that he came to your apartment specifically to kill you," the detective to my right repeats.

I grit my teeth and growl one more time. "No. I didn't."

"But you approached the door with a loaded shotgun," the second detective repeats. "You stated that you were prepared to shoot him if he entered your apartment. You would have killed him. You realize that, don't you?"

I look up just enough to glare at him. "You're damn right I would have killed him. If he went so far as to break into my apartment, I could have assumed he was coming to harm me or Leila. You bet your ass I would have shot him. I wish I had and you can't tell me I did anything wrong by arming myself because he *did* come to the apartment to kill us—both of us. He would have if Leila hadn't gotten to him when she did."

Jim spreads his hands again. "No one is saying you did anything wrong by arming yourself."

"Then what exactly are you saying? Why the hell am I here being questioned by you? He shot me and would have killed Leila. She hit him in self-defense and I know she's already stated that she wasn't trying to kill him—which is a damn sight better than he deserved. So....unless you plan to charge me with something, we're finished here."

"We're finished here for now," Jim tells me, "but we need you to testify before the inquiry."

I throw up my hands, mutter, "Whatever," and walk out.

I storm downstairs fuming. Those sons of bitches better not make it out that either Leila or I did anything wrong when Damon broke into my apartment.

I'm going to have to hurt somebody if the Police try to go after Leila for killing Damon. How dare they even suggest I shouldn't have armed myself or that she shouldn't have hit him the way she did?

My nightmare becomes complete when I get to the garage. I don't see Leila anywhere. The other two detectives stand on opposite sides of the garage questioning Chris and Danny.

I don't have to wonder what they're talking about. I've never seen Danny this furious, but in typical Danny fashion, he doesn't blow up. That isn't his style.

He narrows his blue eyes at the detective in front of him. The guy doesn't know Danny well enough to realize just how dangerous Danny can get when he's mad.

Danny answers the detective's questions through gritted teeth and Danny keeps his lips pinched tight shut except when he absolutely has to open them to say something.

The detective doesn't notice a thing. He keeps his body language casual and even smiles at Danny like they're passing the time of day. I almost pity the detective having to question my brother.

The rest of the crew crowds close to the supply cabinets. John stands over there with them in what looks like a guarding posture. It couldn't be more obvious that the crew is being kept in one place until their turns come to get questioned about Damon's behavior at the pool hall.

The Police Department has even brought in four uniformed officers to stand guard over the crew. How the Police Department sprang this on the whole firehouse is beyond me—or *why* the Police Department sprang this on the whole firehouse. This better not be some backhanded form of intimidation.

The minute I show up, John gestures for me to join the rest of the crew. I go over there and stand with the others while we wait for the detectives to finish with Chris and Danny. Then the others will have to take their turns.

Leila comes downstairs a few minutes later. She looks petrified, but she's holding it together as well as she can.

She comes over to our group and I put my arm around her shoulders. "You okay?" I whisper.

She nods, but she won't look at me. Her wide eyes dart around the firehouse without seeing anything.

I cast a wary glance toward Danny, but right then, the detective finishes questioning him. Danny breaks away and storms back to our group.

The rest of the crew obviously saw the same signs I did. The crew moves out of his way and no one tries to talk to him or even look at him. They all give him a wide berth.

It will take him a while to cool down—and by a while, I mean maybe the rest of the damn day. He can joke around and play the clown all day long, but Danny doesn't forgive and he doesn't forget when someone crosses him.

Fortunately, the Fates smile on us and the fire alarm goes off right at that moment. Chris walks off in the middle of her conversation and the officers don't stop us from loading into the trucks.

No one says a word until the rescue truck pulls out of the garage. Now we can all go back to doing our jobs the way we're supposed to, but Leila and I still have this inquiry hanging over our heads. Will the Police Department try to pull another fast one there, too?

Chapter 20: Leila

I squirm in my uniform, but I can't get comfortable no matter what I do. I glance over my shoulder toward the courtroom behind me.

I'll be going in there to testify in the inquiry into Damon Cassidy's death. I don't know if I can do this. "This is bad!" I choke. "I'm a nervous wreck!"

"Take it easy and just keep breathing," Keith murmurs to me in an undertone. "Just get through this. It will be over soon and we can put this whole thing behind us."

I look up at him, but I don't dare to voice all the fears running through my head. What if we *don't* get through it? What if the Police Department decides to charge me for Damon's murder? What will I do then?

Why would the Police Department hold this inquiry at all if they didn't doubt that I killed Damon in self-defense? Why would they tell me one thing and then change it afterward? What possible evidence could they have come up with to change their determination?

Keith doesn't say it, but I see the same questions haunting his eyes. He doesn't fidget as much as I do and he doesn't glance around as much, but when he does, I see him doubting the outcome as much as I do.

We've cooperated with the Police as much as possible and they already have video footage from both of Damon's attacks, including the one where I killed him. Isn't that enough?

Keith takes a step toward me and rubs his hands up and down my arms. My stiff dress uniform jacket makes it difficult to feel his touch. I really wish I could.

"I'll be right with you," he whispers. "Whatever happens to you in there, it will happen to both of us. We're going through this together. Understand?"

I nod at nothing, and when I still can't bring myself to look at him, he folds his arms around me and pulls me into his chest.

He wears his dress uniform, too. Decorations of every kind cover the front of his chest. He's one of the most decorated firefighters in Howe Fire Department history.

He looks stunning in his uniform with his wet hair combed back. Wearing his hair like that makes his scar stand out even more. Everyone will be able to see it and the Police Department has Keith's medical records in evidence, too.

I just don't understand any of this. I really wish I could appreciate him hugging me right now, but my nerves get ready to snap as we both turn to enter the courtroom.

Keith opens the door for me. A bunch of people in civilian dress sit in the gallery. I don't recognize any of them, but an older lady with greying hair sits in the front row. She sniffles into her handkerchief and dabs her eyes.

Damon told me his mother lived near Howe, but he never took me to meet her. Is that her? Is she the one pressuring the Police Department to hold a formal inquiry into Damon's death?

That thought gives me a little more courage. I pass up the aisle, through the gallery, to the front of the courtroom.

Mark Chesterfield, the Fire Department's legal counsel, sits at the table where the defendant usually sits. I don't want to go over there. The Police Department hasn't officially charged me with anything, but no one has to tell me that I'm the defendant here.

Mark comes toward me and sticks out his hand. "How you doing? Thanks for coming in. Don't worry about any of this. Everything is going to be okay."

I really wish everyone would stop saying that—as if Keith and I had any choice about coming to testify at this inquiry.

Mark escorts us to the table. I've never felt guiltier than when I step behind it.

Keith isn't under any suspicion, but he steps behind the table and takes his place next to me. Mark rattles off a bunch of legal jargon in our ears, but I don't hear a thing.

My gaze rivets to the other table where four Police officers in immaculate dress uniforms assemble to conduct the prosecution's side of the inquiry. They all look so much more intimidating than Mark does. He's too friendly to intimidate anyone.

Keith stiffens and quickly pushes me to the far end of the table. He changes places with me to position himself between me and the Police Department representatives, but that only makes me feel worse.

Mark bends over folders full of notes that he takes out of his briefcase. He says, "If we could just go over a few things first……" but right then, something else distracts me.

The courtroom entrance doors open again and a handful of civilians enter. They separate to sit in the gallery….and then John walks in. He wears his dress uniform, too, and then Danny follows him.

Danny is as decorated as Keith and the three brothers all look incredibly impressive, but not as impressive as the whole firehouse staff filing in behind Danny.

Chris, Billy, Caleb, George, Vince, Sophie, Drew, Naomi.....they're all here and all dressed to the nines in their dress uniforms with all their decorations on display. Even the on-duty crew is here.

They stride in at the back of the courtroom and everyone in the gallery turns around to stare. Even the Police representatives at the prosecutor's table turn around.

Damon's mom—if that's what she is—gawks with her mouth open as John strides to the front of the room, stops at one of the lines of seats, and stands aside while every single last one of my crewmates file in behind him.

They take up three full rows of seats right behind the defense table where Keith, Mark, and I stand. Civilians scamper out of the way to give the firefighters all the space they need to sit together.

They remain standing until everyone gets into place. Then John and Danny slot into the two seats closest to the aisle.

The fire crew stands there at attention for a split second and then they all sit down at the same time. They make plenty of noise and none of them tries to soften the blow.

Their presence changes the whole atmosphere in the courtroom. I never expected them to come out to support me and Keith. None of them let on that they were planning this.

Now that they're here, I don't feel like the defendant anymore—or not the sole defendant.

If the Police Department wants to charge me with murder, they'll be charging the whole Fire Department. That's what the crew's presence means. They're here to back up me and Keith.

My throat constricts. I don't know how I'll testify with so much gratitude overwhelming me, but right then, the judge enters. The bailiff calls, "This hearing will come to order! The Honorable Justice Patricia Ann Henley presiding."

The judge sits down and everyone else sits down at the same time. Mark signals me and Keith to sit down with him and the gallery settles to listen.

The judge is a middle-aged woman with her jet-black hair pulled into a tight, painted-on, sleek bun without a hair out of place.

She has a very long, bony, horsy face with prominent teeth. She looks like a real battleaxe. I can tell she doesn't plan to take any static or cut anyone any slack in this hearing.

I can't decide if that's a good thing or a bad thing, but I don't have a chance before she faces the courtroom. She nods first to the prosecutor's table and then toward us.

"Commander Danilov—Lieutenant Chesterfield—this is the investigatory inquiry into the death of Police Constable Damon Cassidy....."

The lady in the gallery starts sniffling loudly again, but the judge ignores her.

"Begin your opening statements, gentlemen," she orders.

The first officer from the prosecution table stands up. That must be Commander Danilov—the guy who will be representing the Police Department.

"Thank you, Your Honor," he begins. "This panel will present evidence that Police Constable Damon Cassidy conducted a campaign of domestic violence against Firefighter Paramedic Lieutenant Leila Cunningham that included harassment, assault, and threats of bodily harm against her and others in public venues in front of dozens of witnesses. The Police Department will also present evidence that, in the final days of his life, Police Constable Damon Cassidy invaded Lieutenant Cunningham's home and carried out a violent assault against her that put her in the hospital for four weeks and nearly cost her her life."

I stare at the side of Commander Danilov's face while he addresses the court. Did I just hear that right? The Police Department—Damon's Police Department—they're the ones who will present evidence that he was violent? Aren't they going to blame me for this—for anything?

"The Police Department will present video footage showing this attack against Lieutenant Cunningham as well as video footage of the attack that resulted in his death. Constable Cassidy himself carried out this attack and instigated Lieutenant Cunningham to defend herself. The Police Department executed an arrest warrant against Constable Cassidy for his assault against Lieutenant Cunningham, and when he posted bail and regained his freedom, he tracked her down with the intent to kill her in revenge for the crime of ending their relationship."

He waves toward our table. I can't breathe. My mind doesn't want to believe I'm really hearing this.

"After her release from the hospital where she was treated for severe head injuries, Lieutenant Cunningham did not feel safe returning to her own home where Constable Cassidy had carried out this heinous attack. He had also previously threatened and blocked her from entering her own home when she informed him that their relationship was over. Therefore, following her release from the hospital, Lieutenant Cunningham sought refuge with her friend and colleague Firefighter Lieutenant Keith Brewer. Lieutenant Cunningham was staying with Lieutenant Brewer when Constable Cassidy used explosives to invade Lieutenant Brewer's residence, shot him in the head, and would have killed Lieutenant Cunningham if she hadn't subdued him first. Constable Cassidy died of his injuries. Lieutenant Chesterfield and I agree in recommending that Constable Cassidy's death be ruled the result of reasonable self-defense on Lieutenant Cunningham's part and all suspicion of criminal wrongdoing be dismissed with prejudice."

I can't force myself to blink. He did not just say all that. He didn't even mention me and Keith being in a relationship. Commander Danilov didn't say a word about me triggering Damon's first attack by telling him that I'd just spent the night with Keith.

Do all these people plan to gloss that over? Will they ever bring it up at all—or that I was spending the night at Keith's as his new.....whatever I am?

The judge doesn't see anything out of the ordinary in Commander Danilov's introduction. "Very well, Commander," she replies. "Present your evidence."

Commander Danilov and his support staff from the Police Department show both pieces of video footage—the Skype footage of Damon attacking me and the footage from Keith's apartment showing Damon's second attack.

Then Commander Danilov spends an insane amount of time going through all the Police records to establish the whole timeline going all the way back to when Damon assaulted me and threatened Keith outside the firehouse.

I struggle to contain my agitation as the so-called prosecution's case goes on and on and on. I can't deny anymore that the Police Department really is on my side. They're presenting the same case Mark Chesterfield planned to present. They even agreed on it beforehand.

My whole idea of this inquiry gets flipped on its head, but the situation takes a sharp detour when it comes time for Mark to present his case.

He calls me to the stand and walks me through every excruciating detail of my relationship with Damon. I have to recount all the incidents of intimidation, threats, and violence going all the way back to when we first started dating. Then I have to detail all the events Commander Danilov just presented.

Mark calls Keith next and then my world comes screeching to a halt when Mark calls each and every single member of the Fire Department to testify.

They all recount the events at the pool hall and Sophie, Jessie, George, Cameron, and Drew tell how it felt to get called to my house and see me on the floor in a pool of blood.

I start crying silently when Vince takes the stand and tells about how he knew Damon was violent toward women.

Vince looks down at his hands and mumbles in an undertone through his testimony. "I went to school with him. He dated a bunch of women who accused him of slapping them around, controlling their movements, and one of them even said he forced her to break off contact with her brothers and sisters. I saw his relationship with Leila going the same way....."

"Why didn't you warn her?" Mark asks. "She's your friend and a member of your crew. Why didn't you tell her about Damon before they got involved?"

"I didn't find out about it until they'd already been together for two months. I guess he'd already suspected me of keeping an eye on him. Maybe he saw how close the fire crew was and wanted to keep it hidden so I wouldn't warn her. I don't know. By the time I found out, it was already too late." He looks up at me and his eyes glaze with agonized emotion. "I'm sorry. I should have done more to help you. I never should have let this happen....."

He chokes on the last words. I can't see him anymore through my tears. I want to hug him and tell him it isn't his fault. He couldn't have stopped Damon. I probably wouldn't have listened to Vince anyway. I was too set on Damon then, and once I got into it, I found it nearly impossible to get out.

He steps down and Mark wraps up his presentation. "The Fire Department rests, Your Honor. We agree with Commander Danilov in recommending a finding of self-defense in this case."

"Thank you, Lieutenant," the judge replies. "The court agrees with both of you. Police Constable Damon Cassidy's cause of death is ruled reasonable self-defense with no fault assigned to Lieutenant Cunningham or Lieutenant Brewer. This case is dismissed with prejudice. Thank you, gentlemen."

She strikes her gavel and the bailiff calls, "Court is adjourned. All rise!"

Everyone stands up and I whirl around to throw my arms around Keith. He laughs in my ear, lifts my feet off the floor, and hugs me in front of everyone.

Then we turn to the fire crew. They mob our table all talking, shaking hands, and hugging us one after the other. John shakes hands with Mark.

I lose track of everyone in the gallery. I want to say something to Damon's mom or maybe even to find out if she *is* his mom. I don't know what I would say. I can't exactly apologize for killing Damon. She probably wouldn't appreciate talking to me anyway.

That's when I spot Vince in the crowd. He stands on the other side of the fire crew—as far as he can possibly get from me.

I push my way toward him and put my arms around him without saying anything. I would never let something like this come between us.

I don't have to say anything, and when I straighten up, he struggles to control his features. I squeeze his arms and then we both turn back to the group.

That issue is dead and buried as far as I'm concerned. I don't blame him for what happened with Damon and I hope Vince doesn't blame himself, either.

I'm too happy celebrating with my friends and then John says, "Let's get out of here, people. We'll meet back up at the firehouse." He waves to the on-duty crews. "You folks should change back into your regular uniforms in case you get a real call."

We all file out of the courtroom. A bunch of people stand around the lobby, but I'm too happy and excited to notice them. It's really over. Keith and I really can put this behind us. Now I can finally believe that everything is going to be all right.

Chapter 21: Leila

Keith parks his truck in front of the apartment building and lifts his dress uniform jacket from the back seat. I'm still wearing mine.

"Thank Heaven that's over," he growls. "I was really worried right up until Commander Danilov started talking."

"Me, too. I really didn't want to believe he was trying to defend us."

"Did you see that woman in the front row—the one who kept crying through the whole hearing?"

I spin around. "You saw her? Do you know who she was?"

"I was hoping you could tell me. I thought she might be Damon's mother, but I couldn't be sure."

"I thought the same thing. I know his mother lives in town somewhere. Her behavior made me wonder if she made the Police Department conduct that inquiry in the first place."

"That makes sense. Come on. Let's go inside."

He darts in and kisses me once before he gets out, comes around to my side, and opens my door for me, but he doesn't lead me away to the building immediately.

As soon as he shuts the door, he braces both arms on either side of me, pushes me against the truck, and smothers me in kisses.

I collapse under him. I don't want to go anywhere or think anything or be anything. I just want to be right here, with him. I don't even care if anyone sees me kissing him in my dress uniform.

He pushes his body all the way against me. The muscles of his midsection tighten and he doesn't pull away. He doesn't restrain himself at all as he drills all the way into me.

My body erupts in excitement. Is he going to touch me right here in the parking lot? This is the first time neither of us has had to worry about someone seeing us or thinking anything about us making out in public.

Everyone who matters to us already knows we're together. No one is out to get us. No one is questioning whether we're doing the right thing.

He gives me a playful nip on the lower lip and pulls off my mouth with a loud smack. "Come on," he tells me. "We have a date."

"You mean I have a date with my studly firefighter boyfriend?" I smirk at him. "He is gonna be so jealous."

"That's nothing compared to how jealous I'll be of him." He steals one more kiss and takes my hand. "Behave yourself or else."

I laugh. I don't have to worry about anything Keith does and he won't get jealous of himself. That's the joke.

We go inside and kiss in the elevator until we have to separate to walk to the apartment. He glances up at the security camera while he unlocks the door. He's done that every time he passes under it. I don't blame him. That camera changed both of our lives.

He lets me enter first and then triple-locks the door behind him. That has become a habit for him, too.

I watch him go through the same routine of locking the door and then going to the windows to scan the neighborhood. He does it first thing in the morning, when he returns to the apartment every time he goes out, and multiple times during the day when he's here.

He doesn't slacken his vigilance at all even though Damon is dead. Sometimes Keith's behavior really worries me.

I go into the bedroom, change out of my uniform, and put on my casual clothes before I go to the kitchen and start going through the fridge.

I'm still deciding what to make for dinner when Keith comes out in *his* casual clothes. He looks more relaxed, but he automatically goes straight back to the windows again before he lets himself sit down on the couch.

I put some rice and water into the rice maker and go sit down next to him. He's fiddling with his phone. "So what do you want to do tonight?" I ask him. "My boyfriend is on shift all night, so we can fool around behind his back."

He doesn't take the joke. He leans forward to put his phone on the coffee table, turns to me, and clasps my hand where it lies in my lap. "I want to talk to you."

"About what?"

"About our future together."

"Uh...okay. What is our future together?"

He studies me for a second. Now he's making me nervous.

Before I can move, he pivots sideways on the couch, pulls something out of his pocket, and cracks open a black velvet box in front of me. "Marry me."

My jaw drops. I can't make a sound, not even to ask him what he just said.

He doesn't wait for a response before he takes the ring out and slips it onto my finger. I stare at it with my mouth open. Am I dreaming?

"I don't want to wait anymore," he murmurs. "I want us to be legit. That's what I mean by talking about our future. I want us to go all the way—the house, the kids, the cars, the bank accounts—all of it."

I look up at him in a daze. Did he really just say that?

"Come on!" he exclaims. "What do you say? You know it's right. What are we waiting for, really?"

I open my mouth. "I....uh......"

He frowns slightly and then waves his hand aside. "You don't have to think about it that hard! If you don't want to, just say so. We can sell your house and I'll sell this apartment. We can buy a house closer to the......"

"I already have a house." The words fall out of my mouth before I realize what I'm saying.

He breaks off with his mouth open. Now it's his turn to blink at me. "I know you do. That's why I said...."

"We don't need to buy a house. We already have one."

"Yeah, but......" He blinks again extra slowly. "I thought....you know.....I thought you didn't want to go back there. Isn't that what you said?"

"I said that before. That was when Damon was still alive, but now....." I look back down at the ring. It's definitely real. I'm going to marry Keith Brewer.

My heart turns a somersault and then those words finally sink into my brain. I'm going to marry Keith Brewer. I'm that woman—the lucky woman that got him. He's mine and I'm his. This ring proves it.

"I guess the house means something different to me now," I tell him. "At first, it was the evidence of how badly Damon treated me. I didn't want to see that all the time, but now the house is the evidence of how you and I got together. I wouldn't mind seeing that all the time." I burst into a grin. "In fact, I want to."

"Uh....okay...." he stammers.

"It's a really nice house. It has four bedrooms and a big backyard. It's in a really nice neighborhood—perfect for kids.....and it's within walking distance of the school.....and the park. It's everything we need in a house. We don't need to sell it to buy something else."

He blinks again and says, "Uh....okay....."

I wait for him to say something. He stares at me like he can't believe he's hearing this from me. I definitely want all of that with him—the house, the kids, the cars, the bank accounts—all of it.

All at once, he bursts into a huge grin, lunges for me, and tackles me down on the couch. He crushes me for a second and makes me scream before he jumps off. "Come on!" He grabs my hand. "Let's go over there right now! Let's move in right now—right this minute."

I sit up with difficulty and look at him. "Are you sure?"

"Yeah, absolutely! I couldn't figure out why this place was giving me such a bad vibe. Let's get the hell out of here. I don't want to live here anymore. Let's go."

He tugs me off the couch. He won't leave me alone until he drags me back downstairs and practically throws me into his truck.

"We're going to have to come back here to get all our stuff, you know," I remind him.

He laughs while he turns the ignition. "Right, but not today. God, why didn't you tell me before? I've been climbing the walls in that apartment."

I grin at the side of his face. I haven't seen him this happy since before the shooting. I'm not sure I can remember him this happy even before the shooting.

I knew he was climbing the walls in that apartment. I just didn't think of the solution—until now.

I put on my seatbelt and the ring bites into my finger. I'm going to marry Keith Brewer. I'm wearing his ring right now. We're getting married and we're going to move into my old house—our new house.

He smiles at the road while he drives across town with his elbow hanging out the driver's window. He really is so much more relaxed, now that he's out of that apartment.

He pulls into the driveway of my house, switches off the engine, and gets serious when he squints at the house through the windshield. This is our house now. We'll make it our own.

"Are you sure you want to do this?" he asks. "You don't have to. There are plenty of other perfectly good houses around town."

"No, I want this one. Come on."

I don't wait for him to open my door for me. I hop out, grab his arm, and tow him inside.

No one has cleaned the blood off the carpet since the fire crew extricated me from the living room. "We're definitely going to have to replace that," Keith remarks.

"Other than that, it looks pretty good." I grab the sponge from the kitchen and wipe the dust off the countertop. "And you probably want to redecorate. This isn't as much of a man cave as your apartment."

"My apartment was not a man cave!" he insists.

"This won't be, either. I get veto power over any décor decisions you make."

He goes over to the couch, sits down on it, and wrinkles his nose. "I might bring my leather sofa set over from the apartment."

"Bring anything you want," I tell him.

"So.....wife......" he begins and then busts up laughing at his own joke.

"You better watch it," I tell him.

He looks up at me beaming from ear to ear. I barely recognize him. "Hey....come here. We need to christen this place."

"Christen?" I repeat. "You mean like smash a bottle of champagne against the wall?"

He snorts, stands up, and comes into the kitchen. He sidles up to me, kisses me on the side of the neck, and uses his weight to push me against the counter. "What will it be.....the kitchen counter......the bathroom shower......the back lawn.......the wall......How would you like it for your first time?"

"First time!" I try to laugh it off, but he doesn't let me.

He spins me away from him, uses his bulk to bend me over the kitchen counter, and bites me on the neck from behind. I gasp, and before I can either protest or answer, he dives one meaty hand in front of me and between my legs.

He grips me through my jeans, rakes his other hand up my chest to my neck, and pries my head back.

He presses his mouth against my ear and snarls low into my brain. His hot breath sets my every nerve and cell on fire.

"You're all mine now," he growls. "You can't get away, so don't think your firefighter boyfriend is going to come rescue you....."

I start to laugh, but he's rubbing me so hard between my legs that it comes out as a moan.

He drills into me from behind and feel how hard he is. He screws his bulge into me from behind and pulverizes me against the counter, but his arm still protects me from the granite edge.

"You want that, don't you?" he husks. "You want me to make you mine. Don't you?"

I gasp again and start to pant. He's driving me wild and taking me over the edge way too fast. I can't stop.

I screw my hips down on his hand and he murmurs in satisfaction. "Mmm. Yes, baby. You want that so bad, don't you? Mmmm. You are so hot."

I can't think straight with him rubbing me like this. I don't care where he does it as long as it happens. I would be thrilled to do it in all the places he just mentioned and I'm sure we will.....eventually.

I'm just getting started when he pulls off, turns me around to face him, and he catches my eye once before he starts kissing me endlessly.

I drape my arms around his neck, but I can't think with this buzzing desire coursing through me. I want him to take me right now on the kitchen counter, but he must have some other idea about what christening this place means.

He shoves me back against the counter facing me this time, flexes his knees, and drives up into me from below. He feels so strong and hard and determined. He really wants this and I do, too. I'm just dying of curiosity to find out what he does next.

He steps back and his eyes hold me enthralled. He makes me tremble all over and then time stops when he grabs my waistband to unbutton my jeans.

He doesn't look away once while he slides the zipper down. I gasp out loud and then scream when he crams his hand down the front of my panties. His fingers set my world on fire as he slips inside.

I can't tear my eyes away from his all-powerful gaze. He watches and sees every reaction, every wince and swoon, as he sends me reeling over the edge.

I explode on his fingers. Only his weight pinning me against the counter holds me up and stops me from falling.

He doesn't try to kiss me or touch me in any other way. He just watches me succumb to his attention. I'm his now. Doesn't he see that in my eyes? Can't he hear it in my plaintive screams for him? He holds me in the palm of his hand—literally.

His bicep ripples under his T-shirt with every deep, agonizing thrust. I can't help rotating my hips on his hand. He can feel how wet I am and spasms of rapture clamp down on his fingers.

With no warning at all, he pulls his hand out, takes hold of my jeans, and slides them down. I'm still teetering in the stratosphere somewhere when he kneels down, pulls off my shoes, and holds my jeans cuffs for me to step out of them.

My body obeys him implicitly. My mind completely shuts down. Whatever he wants to do, I won't fight him. I just want him to take me there—again and again and again—forever. Isn't that what this is? Isn't that what marrying him means?

He takes off my shoes, socks, and jeans. I don't have time to think about what he'll do next before he raises his head and plunges face first between my legs.

I scream again and collapse against the kitchen counter, but he grabs both hands behind my ass and steers me into his mouth.

His tongue twines into my deepest core and rocks me off my feet. He uses his face to hold me against the counter and then, in a masterful move of perfect expert control, he grabs my leg behind my knee and lifts it over his shoulder.

Now nothing can stop him from consuming me out of my mind. My hands fly to his hair and I feel his scar under his hair. All those memories make me want him so much more. Each one shines like a jewel to remind me how lucky I am.

His tongue coils and slithers deeper into my being. I can't cope with all the spikes of blissful sensation wiping out every trace of unhappiness and ghostly doubt.

His fingers bore into me again and I dissolve in a torrent of climaxes. He stretches me to the breaking point even as his tongue skyrockets me out of this world.

Just when I think it can't get any more intense, he stands up. Those eyes make me disintegrate in another river of passionate desire. I can't take this, but he's far from done.

He kisses me once, circles me with both arms, and lifts my feet off the floor. He steers my legs around his waist so I have no choice but to cling to him. I'm naked from the waist down and both his hands supporting me can find whatever part of me he wants to enjoy next.

My head falls on his shoulder as I sob and whimper in ecstasy. I want to hide from all this mind-blowing love and passion burning me up, but I should know better than to think he'll let me quit—not yet.

He does something—I don't know what—and then he lowers me onto his shaft. I scream again, and before I can finish spinning out of my mind, he grabs a handful of my hair from behind and drags my head up to look at him.

I drown in his eyes and in all the pleasure pouring into me from him and out of me into him. I can't keep track of everything that's happening. I only know the impossible depths of his eyes holding me captive.

I'll stay here forever, in this majestic sea of loving him. I don't need to know anything else.

He can walk around the house with me like this. He can do it with me anywhere he likes as long as he looks at me like that. Nothing else matters except that we're together here—he and I.

Epilogue: Keith

I crack one of the coolers and check that it still has enough ice in it. Two dozen beer bottles lie nestled inside. None of the ice has melted yet.

John gets my attention by calling across the beach. "Hey, could you get the coals started?"

"Sure," I reply.

I shut the cooler and go over to the barbecue. John kneels by an enormous pile of driftwood that he's collected for our bonfire. Winter is coming and it's going to get cold tonight.

A line of tents already dots the beach. Oakleigh and the other kids run around and play out on the wet sand.

Cameron, his wife Olivia, Jessie, and George go back and forth between the tents and the parking lot bringing sleeping bags, pillows, foam mattresses, and everything else we'll need to camp out on the beach tonight.

This new twist on the old barbecue theme was Leila's idea. She's always coming up with crazy ideas for how to make the firehouse barbecues better, more fun, and even more of a bonding experience for all of us.

Most of the crew dismisses her ideas. In fact, her ideas have become one of the firehouse's standing jokes, but not this time.

Everyone latched onto this one with a vengeance. Now everyone is packing their stuff onto the beach to dig in for an all-night adventure.

My tent sits on the other side of the campsite away from everyone else. I don't know about the rest of these folks, but I want some privacy tonight.

I don't want to get woken up in the middle of the night by Billy snoring, which is what happens when I work the night shift with him and we bunk down in the staff bunk room at the station.

The other worst-case scenario is that someone has to get up in the middle of the night to go to the bathroom, gets disoriented in the dark, walks straight through the wall of someone else's tent, and the whole shebang comes crashing down with the poor, helpless residents trapped inside.

When that happens, I want to be one of the bystanders laughing from the sidelines instead of the chump getting stepped on while they extract themselves from the rubble.

I grin to myself thinking about it while I pour the charcoal into the barbecue, dowse the pile with lighter fluid, and set it alight.

The flames catch just as John puts a match to his pile of driftwood. Oakleigh and the other kids come over to watch it all go up in smoke.....and then they notice the toffees in the bowl on the picnic table. It sure took the munchkins long enough to find the candy.

"Hey, Keith!" Oakleigh calls. "These are the same toffees I gave you in the hospital."

"They're just the same brand," I yell back. "I ate those long ago. I got a new package for tonight."

She unwraps one of the candies, sticks it in her mouth, and runs off to play with her friends. These kids are so gullible.

John shoots me a knowing grin and heads over to the parking lot just as Ellen comes down from their car. She carries two sleeping bags in each hand with two plastic shopping bags looped over her wrists.

It doesn't work out too well because her leg brace digs into the sand with every step. She doesn't have any trouble walking on solid asphalt, but she finds it hard to balance on the sand.

John goes over to her and takes everything out of her hands. "I'll take that. Maybe you can help Keith get the steaks ready for the barbecue."

"I don't need any help getting the steaks ready for the barbecue!" I interrupt. "I'm a man. I can handle barbequing without a woman's supervision."

Ellen laughs. "Then how about I stand by and admire your technique?"

"Now you're talking." I point to one of the bags resting on the ground nearby. "How about you polish my surgical instruments while you're at it, too?"

She laughs again. "You got it."

John disappears up to the car and replaces her in trucking all their stuff down to their tent. He's just going back for his third load when the rescue truck angles into the parking lot from the main road.

I try not to get too excited, but when the crew unloads, I wave to Leila across the beach. Now the party really starts. The ambulance crews pull in next and everybody joins in to help set up camp.

Leila carries four loaded shopping bags to the picnic table and then comes over to give me a kiss. "How's the Master Chef at work?"

"I'm good, now that I got my trusty assistant helping me. I'm just about to anesthetize the patient before I make the first incision."

She laughs and Ellen brings me a pair of tongs from the bag. She rests the shaft of the tongs on her wrist and bows from the waist as best she can as she presents me my implement of destruction with great pomp and ceremony. "Your scalpel, Doctor."

"Thank you, Nurse. Prepare the suction."

Danny comes over and claps me on the shoulder. "You won't believe the call you just missed."

"Did you fall over and get your foot stuck up your ass?" I ask and everyone standing around explodes.

Danny joins in their laughter and then says, "That was last week. No, just now we attended a call where a guy got thrown from a horse and literally got his head stuck in a tree. Like, his head was through the tree and the rest of him was hanging by the neck toward the ground."

"Quit fooling around!" I chide. "I swear, how do you come up with the wildest crap every time you tell one of these stories?"

"It's true," Leila tells me. "He isn't making it up. That really was the call."

I stare at her. "You're serious."

She nods. "The guy was doing a steeple chase run and the horse balked at one of the jumps. The guy flew through the air and his head went between two limbs of the tree trunk right where they parted. He fell down and his neck got wedged right in the crotch of these two trunks. He was hanging there like a......"

She trails off while she searches for the right words.

"Like a ragdoll," Danny finishes.

She points at him. "Yes! Thank you."

"So his head didn't actually go *through* the tree," I correct.

"Yes, it did," Chris tells me. "It took us almost an hour to get him unstuck."

"And there were branches all over the place," Leila adds. "There was at least as much wood and vegetation above him as there was on all other sides. He was as through the tree as he possibly could be."

"Dang," I exclaim. "That must have hurt."

Cameron joins us just in time to hear the story. "Was he still conscious?"

"Was he ever!" Danny counters. "He was yelling his flippin' head off."

"I bet he was," I remark.

I glance down at the coals just then. They're ready, so I use a stick to break them apart, spread them into a nice glowing bed, and place the grill over them.

"Do you need any help with that?" Danny asks me.

I jab my tongs at him. "Keep away if you don't want to get hurt."

They all laugh and I get busy putting the steaks on the grill. A few people gather around John's bonfire, which is blazing away nicely now.

Leila sidles over to me and puts her arm around the back of my waist. She looks up and kisses me. "How was your day?"

"It was great. I finished bracing the back porch so it isn't a health and safety hazard anymore."

"Thank you. We wouldn't want the pitter-patter of tiny feet to punch through the rotten wood and get hurt, would we?"

I look down at her and get a thrill of adrenaline when I see the look in her eyes. No one knows our little secret. She's pregnant, but we decided to keep it quiet until she gets a little farther along.

Meanwhile, I've been spending every spare minute fixing up the house. We have a lot more to do to child-proof it before someone starts toddling around the place and falling over every electric wire we leave lying on the floor.

Childish laughter and a few screams draw our attention to the beach. Oakleigh, Cameron's kids Felix and Ainsley, and all the other firehouse kids have run into the waves. They're out there tackling each other, pushing each other's heads underwater, and thrashing around while they struggle for dominance.

Leila pulls me closer and rests her head on my shoulder while we both watch. We're seeing a vision of our future in front of us right now. It's going to be a beautiful future and I can't wait.

Ellen, Chris, Olivia, and the other women set the picnic table and put out potato salad, chips, and all the condiments for the steaks, burgers, hotdogs, and sausages.

I take the first batch of steaks off the coals and Leila carries them to the table. Ellen comes back to help me lay out the burger patties and then she has to go supervise Oakleigh and the kids getting their food without making a mess of things.

Leila gets more involved than usual, not just with Ellen and Oakleigh, but with the kids in general. She never did that before.

I can't help but get another flutter in my chest. A lot of things are going to change in the next few years. Our lives won't look like anything we can recognize.

The sun has completely set by the time everyone gets fed and biting cold sets in over the beach. Some of the kids start crying. They have to change out of their wet clothes before they can crawl into their sleeping bags and go to sleep.

The rest of us gather around the bonfire. I sit down on a driftwood log and Leila sits on my lap. No one looks twice at us acting affectionately with each other. Everyone is used to it by now.

Leila drapes one arm behind my neck and rests her head against my skull. I want to nuzzle into her neck, but that might be more than the crew is comfortable with. I can wait until I get her into the tent.

She smells different since we found out she's pregnant. She might never go back to smelling the way she did before. That might be one of the many things that will never go back to the way they were before. That list is getting mighty long lately.

We listen to the crew talking late into the night, but neither Leila nor I join in. This moment is enough—just us enjoying good company and the bliss of being alive.

End of Book 2.

Keep Reading

F irehouse Blues Series: Book 3: Burned Out

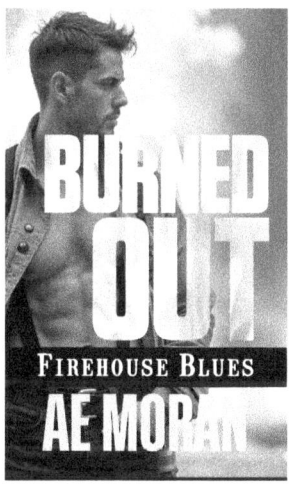

Firefighter Danny Brewer has it all—stunning good looks, a kickass sense of humor, and a job he loves. He's been decorated for heroism in the line of duty as a firefighter and he has the scars to prove it. The scars on the inside cut worse than the scars on the outside, though, and there is one thing Danny doesn't have—a woman and a family to share his life with.

All that is about to change when a single mother and her son move into the house next door. When the boy knocks on Danny's door to see if any kids live there, that one innocent visit will set off a chain reaction that will leave all their lives in ruins. Can Danny save his new family before disaster tears them apart?

You can find it at your favorite book retailer.

Get All of AE Moran's Free Books

S ign Up Once—Get all A.E. Moran's free books including brand new releases

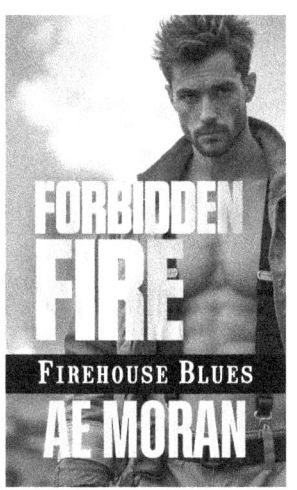

When what you want most is the one thing you can never have......

Austin McAuliffe is every woman's dream firefighter—young, strong, drop-dead hot, and selflessly dedicated to his career—and to the woman of his heart, Emma Brady. Only one other person holds a place in Austin's life—his best friend and fellow firefighter, Theo Gough. Austin insists on Theo spending time with Austin and Emma as a couple, especially when these two firefighters have a hard day at the office.

No one can believe when Austin completely flips out and randomly accuses Theo and Emma of flirting with each other in front of the whole fire crew. Could there be some deeper, more sinister reason for Austin to suddenly lose his mind and lash out at those closest to him?

Emma is devastated when Austin coldly dumps her with no warning and disappears out of her life, but Austin casts a long shadow. The nightmare of his sudden betrayal will come back to haunt Emma and Theo long after Austin is gone. Will the ghosts of the past ruin any chance for them to regain their happiness.....or will Austin's madness take down everyone he cares about along with him?

Sign up at www.authoraemoran.com to read it for free.

About AE Moran

A.E Moran is the contemporary romance pen name for Theo Mann.

I write 70 books per year—and yes, before you ask, all these books are my original creative work. Nothing written under my name is AI-generated or ghostwritten because I write better than AI and any ghostwriter out there.

People don't read fiction for entertainment or to escape from reality. People read fiction to see their humanity reflected in another person's character and story.

This is my promise to you. When you read my books, you'll see your own humanity reflected in the characters and stories. I take this commitment to my readers very seriously. My books are an intimate form of communication between us. I would never disrespect my readers by turning that over to a machine or another writer. This is my bond between me and you as my reader.

I write 20,000 words per day as my daily work output. If anyone with a public platform would like to challenge me to prove this in a controlled environment, feel free to contact me on this website's contact page.

I worked as a professional ghostwriter for fifteen years. Now I'm going for the Guinness World Record by writing 700 books over the next ten years and 1400 books over the next twenty years, all originally written by me. See my website for the full book list.

I'm also the author of *Proof for the Existence of God* and the *Crimes Against Fiction* blog. You can find all my nonfiction work at www.crimes-against-fiction.com.

If you have a story idea, or if you would like me to explore a series in more depth, or if you'd like me to explore a character by writing a spinoff series about that character or world, leave me a message on my website's contact page. I answer all reader emails, so ask me anything, tell me what you liked and didn't like, and let me know where you'd like your favorite series to go. I would love to hear your ideas and find out what you'd like to read next.

You can find out more at www.theomann.com or at www.authoraemoran.com.

Also by AE Moran (so far)

<u>Standalone Novels</u>

Heart on a Knife Edge

Dream Dimension

Just Friends

Back From the Dead

Damaged

Small Town Reunion

<u>Series</u>

Firehouse Blues (Books 1-10)

Turning Point Ranch (Books 1-10)

The Billionaires' Club (Books 1-10)